Joe [illegible handwritten inscription]

PROVERBS 3:5-6

LOST AND FOUND

A Novel

By

JOE NILSEN

LOST AND FOUND
by Joe Nilsen

Printed in the United States of America

ISBN 978-1-60647-783-0

Unless otherwise indicated, Bible quotations are taken from the New Revised Standard Version of the Bible. Copyright © 1989 by Thomas Nelson, Inc.

www.xulonpress.com

Dedicated to my God-given companion

on earth. Her name is Evy.

Summer, 2008

As a reader I have been a fan of adventure and intrigue most of my life. These days there are many wonderful writers who weave their story-lines and entertain us with the feats of unusual heroes, who always seem to triumph over the bad guys in the end. The backgrounds of these protagonists are often shrouded in mystery – it's part of their charm.

In *Lost and Found* I have taken a different approach with my "hero," Ned Reed. If I succeed, you will know all that makes him the complex man that he is. Part of this uniqueness is his spirituality. His faith in God is an on-going theme, and it serves as a backdrop for all his life experiences and moral choices.

Can Ned figure out the contradictions of his life? What about the women in his life? And, will he prevail against the bad guys?

Sorry, you'll have to read on………

"One life on this earth is all that we get, whether it is enough or not enough, and the obvious conclusion would seem to be that at the very least we are fools if we do not live it as fully and bravely and beautifully as we can."

— Frederick Buechner

"For surely I know the plans I have for you, says the Lord, plans for your welfare and not for harm, to give you a future with hope."

— From the prophet Jeremiah, Chapter 29, verse 11

CHAPTER ONE

I t was a dark and stormy night......but that's another story. Actually it was just after dawn and the rays of the sun cast a broad band of color across the sea, like a beckoning road leading to some unknown place.

Ned Reed stood on the balcony outside his bedroom contemplating this sight which had greeted him almost every morning for seven months. The only difference today was a breeze signaling the subtle change of seasons in this paradise which he called home.

San Marcos was still a hidden treasure in the Caribbean. It was one of the last of a chain of islands that included the tourist *meccas* of Sint Maarten, St. Kitts, and St. Lucia. But it was a good thirty miles east of its closest neighbor in the Lesser Antilles. There was no airport on the island, not even a landing strip. That factor, and its relatively small size, just sixteen square miles, had guarded its anonymity and discouraged developers from investing their millions in yet another tropical play station. The residents had every intention of preserving their way of life, to resist all efforts to change the character of their little bit of heaven on earth.

Most of the islands in the region were colonized and exploited by the British, the Dutch and the French over the centuries. San Marcos' population, however, could trace their origins directly to the survivors of three Spanish galleons which had been wrecked and sunk off its eastern coast during a vicious hurricane in the 1700's.

Though beautiful, this speck in the ocean was anything but a land of milk and honey to the first inhabitants. Only the presence of several natural springs and some edible vegetation enabled them to survive. Hopes of rescue gradually faded, and a hardy but graceful life developed on the island. San Marcos' early history was mostly folklore reflecting the courage and industry of those early settlers. Undoubtedly their feats were heightened with the retelling of the stories from one generation to the next.

To the ancestors of those first adventurers, about 2,000 strong, most of whom shared no more than a dozen surnames, was added an assortment of mavericks who chose to seek their own anonymity in this place, where folks were inclined to live and let live.

Standing there looking out at the timeless sea, Ned acknowledged that the restlessness that brought him here was still very much a part of him. There had been many dark and stormy nights in his life. This move to San Marcos was to begin a new chapter, a change of course, a mid-life correction, a cleansing of his soul. Perhaps, he thought, I need to follow this golden road elsewhere.

Ned Reed, alias John Henry, spent most of his days in a predictable routine. In his mid-forties, he was in remarkably good shape. At 200 pounds there was not an ounce of fat on his 6'2" frame. A deep tan contrasted with a full head of sandy hair, streaked by the tropical sun. The only hint of age was the "crows- feet" defining his sky-blue eyes. When he was on the beach, if you looked closely, you would notice scars from long-healed wounds on his upper torso and back. Each scar testified to a life that had seen its share of danger and brushes with death.

After cereal and a bowl of fruit he set out on his daily bike ride. One pronounced feature of San Marcos was a road that encircled its entire shoreline. It provided a breath-taking view of the ocean from any vantage point. It gently rose and fell according to the contours of the land. For some unknown reason it had never been given a name. Everyone just referred to it as "The Belt."

Ned could afford any bicycle he desired, but he preferred the very same ten-speed that he purchased when he was in college. For more than twenty-five years he had maintained it in perfect working condition. It was becoming more of a challenge to replace worn-out parts, but he learned to improvise with those from similar brands. When gear cables frayed, he made new ones himself.

The Belt had little traffic at any time of the day or night. There were very few motor vehicles on the island and most people congregated in the major residential areas on the east and west coasts. Small farms dotted the fertile plateau which dominated the island's interior. There were stretches where Ned wouldn't see any sign of civilization for miles.

It was on these morning treks that Ned did his best thinking. It usually cleared his mind – but not this morning. He had awakened in a somber mood, but the physical exertion of the ride did not change it. In fact, it was intensifying. Something deep within was warning him that something was about to happen that would change all of his plans....again.

After storing his bike in the area assigned to his unit, Ned showered, shaved and donned his customary khaki shorts and Yankees tee shirt. He took his laptop out onto the balcony and spent the next two hours journaling. This is how he spent six mornings a week since he arrived on San Marcos. The seventh morning, Sunday, he hiked the narrow road over the plateau to a small Roman Catholic mission where he attended Mass. Fluent in Spanish, and several other languages, he joined the others in the usual responses. He was almost always the only Anglo there, and stood a good eight inches taller than the priest, who had to reach up to place the communion wafer in his mouth. They shook hands at the door each Sunday after the Mass, but not a word was ever spoken between them. Their eyes would meet, and it was as if the cleric really knew him and the reason for his being there.

Afternoons were spent soaking in the healing rays of the sun at the largely deserted beach in the cove (*Dermatologists: just read on*). He would swim laps across the tranquil inlet, and then settle into a book from one of his favorite authors: Kellerman, Mitchner, Grisham, Child, Nouwen, Manning, and Merton.

Such a daily routine would have driven the average person to distraction after a few days or a few weeks, but Ned had had enough adventure to last a lifetime. This was his chosen time to be grounded, to enjoy the luxury of introspection, and to consider how he wanted to invest the next half of his life. This was why the sense of foreboding that had invaded his psyche all day was so disconcerting.

Arriving back at the apartment just before six he took another quick shower, put on slacks and a sport shirt, and headed down to the seaside. The shops would just be closing and the cantinas reopening. Most people preferred to sit outside under colorful umbrellas, cooled by the gentle breezes that wafted in from the sea. Ned could hardly remember ever seeing a fly or mosquito on San Marcos. He had heard that it was due to the release of an airborne substance from a certain tree which was native to the island.

Ned chose to dine at Pablo's, his favorite eatery on the island. The owner/maitre de/waiter sat him at his usual spot, facing the entrance. His need to sit in full view of things was a vestige from a life he had lived for so long, where vigilance was necessary and at times death-defying. Three or four tables were occupied by couples. At a large table in the rear, near the swinging kitchen door, sat a plump woman with three young children. This was Pablo's family. Ned had seen them on several occasions. The wife made eye contact with him and waved.

The food on San Marcos was tasty. The fish was always fresh, supplemented by local produce and fresh breads baked daily. Meats and other items were brought in every few days by boat from neighboring islands. Ned ordered a salad and some of Pablo's great fish stew. As he was finishing his salad he noted an attractive young woman as she entered the restaurant. She was seated at a far table but facing him. *Definitely not a San Marcan*, he thought. Probably in her mid-thirties, she had auburn hair pulled back in a casual ponytail. She was slim, but not overly so, and wore a yellow sun dress. Her complexion was radiant, her skin pale, as if she had never spent any time in the sun (*Dermatologists may now applaud*).

There had been many beautiful women who crossed Ned's path in these months. Some had even made overtures to him. But that had been an aspect of his life that he had placed on hold. Yet now he found himself unable to look away from this delicate beauty. And it was more than her physical appearance. She was ill at ease. In this otherwise tranquil atmosphere she was fidgeting. She barely acknowledged Pablo as he placed a glass of water in front of her. And her eyes darted nervously around the room.

Suddenly the hairs on Ned's neck seemed to stand on end as dormant instincts were awakened. Glancing at the entrance he caught sight of the barrel of a gun. In one leap he covered the distance from his table to the door. Throwing himself into the air he collided with a figure just as the deafening sound of a gunshot erupted. His momentum carried the two of them outside on to the sidewalk. The assailant regained his balance first and quickly hopped on the back of a motor scooter and disappeared around the corner.

Reentering the cantina Ned found the other patrons in various states of disarray. Pablo's children were screaming.

Their father was already on the phone summoning the police. The young woman almost knocked Ned over as she headed for the exit. Reflexively, he grasped her arm but she slipped away. He looked at his hand and it was full of blood. Recovering quickly he chased her and caught her three buildings away. He held her tightly until she stopped resisting. He could feel the strength drain from her body.

In Spanish he said, "You're hurt. Don't worry, help is on the way."

She just stared at him, so he repeated himself in English adding, "The police will be here soon."

"No police," she said desperately. "They can't help me. No one can help me."

At that moment Ned Reed knew that his self-imposed exile had ended.

CHAPTER TWO

Staten Island, New York: April 15, 1972

Ten year-old Ned Reed was on top of the world. It was a secure world. Growing up in the sixties was not so turbulent for a boy who belonged to a loving family on another island, this one within sight of Lower Manhattan. Political assassinations, a controversial war, campus protests, and the emerging drug culture were far from his concern. That was for the adults in his life to worry about.

Ned's world consisted of home, school, church, and the "fort", a makeshift clubhouse built from scrap lumber in the woods behind the development of modest Cape Cod style dwellings. From this, their headquarters, he and his neighborhood buddies launched their own war games, but there were never any permanent casualties. It was where they did their male-bonding, far from the feminine side of the species. None of them were ready to openly admit curiosity in that regard.

He was a fifth grader at P.S. 30, a short walk from home. He enjoyed school, especially science, and just this year began learning to play the trumpet. Mr. Sussman, the band teacher, told him that he was doing so well that by September he would be able to join the school orchestra. It wasn't exactly the New York Philharmonic, but then Ned knew that he would never be a Dizzy Gillespie either.

Staten Island was changing, but it was still unique among the five boroughs of the City of New York. Broad boulevards connected small, seemingly self-contained communities. Only nine miles wide and fifteen long, it contained many parks and nature trails, thousands of acres of undeveloped land, and even a few small vegetable farms. The Island even had its own beaches along the south shore, and an amusement park which operated all summer until Labor Day weekend.

Until the Verrazano-Narrows Bridge opened in 1964, this cozy isle could only be reached from the rest of New York by boat. Every weekday morning ferries departed every fifteen minutes from the port of St. George, carrying 3,000 commuters on each passage. They went right by the Statue of Liberty to the Battery at the southern tip of Manhattan. Every evening the business and bustle of the "city" was left behind on the return voyage home.

The completion of the bridge to Brooklyn and its connecting arteries changed the face of Staten Island, but the new expressways carried mostly cars with New Jersey license plates, as well as interstate truckers bringing their wares to the city that never slept. Most Islanders who worked in Manhattan still crowded the ferry terminal each morning. It was the greatest bargain in the world, a nickel each way. Ned's older sister Kara had joined that throng the year before after graduating from high school. She had landed a job as a secretary at a small brokerage firm just a short walk from the ferry. She didn't like that title, "secretary". She and her co-workers were already referring to themselves as "administrative assistants." They were clearly ahead of their time.

Yes, Ned's world was very secure. His dad, John Reed, was an Episcopal priest, serving a parish with its origins back to the 1700's. Now in its third building it still retained the architecture and aura of a much earlier time. It was like a second home to the youngest of the Reed children. He often popped in after school to see what his father might be doing. Sometimes Ned would just sit for a time alone in the sanctuary, taking in the Biblical themes depicted in the ornate stained-glass windows. Sometimes he imagined himself standing up in front like his father. He loved and respected him. So did the people of St. Simon's Church. He was a caring man and an outstanding preacher. He came there right out of seminary, and was still there twenty-three years later.

Anita Reed, nee Randolph, Ned's mom, was a 5'2" dynamo. Everyone called her Nita. She always wanted to be called Anita, but eventually gave up correcting all those who thought they were being affectionate by using her nickname. It's why she gave her three children names that could stand on their own: Brian, Kara, and Ned. Anita was a pediatric nurse when she met John on a blind date, and had kept up her license and skills by working every other weekend at St. Vincent's Medical Center. That's where all the kids were born.

Brian, thirteen years his senior, was a Marine in his second tour of duty in Viet Nam, where he was a guard at the U.S. Embassy in Saigon. There had been some talk recently at the dinner table about his possibly coming home again soon. The difference in ages between the brothers limited their interaction. Brian was already in high school the year that Ned was born.

And then there was Kara. Still living at home at nineteen, she had a large circle of friends who occupied most of her time, especially on weekends. Though Ned's reluctant baby-sitter over the years, she was still a good sport as far as he was concerned. She good-naturedly teased him, occasionally helped him with homework, or bought him a pack of baseball cards at the ferry terminal on her way home from work.

Life was good, very good. But today it would all change – forever.

When he left for school on this particular morning Ned's father was sitting at the dining room table engulfed in receipts and tax forms. It was the annual "Reed Tax Marathon." Hopefully, later that evening the whole family would pile into the car and then they would make their ritual trip to the Post Office. From there it was on to Ralph's for an Italian ice. Ned's grandfather, never a fan of the I.R.S., had once told his youngest grandchild that the only thing certain in life was death and taxes. The boy thought it was an original idea. Little did he know that on this day the meaning of that phrase would be forever etched on his memory.

That afternoon Ned dutifully waited for the crossing guard to stop traffic outside the school. On signal he and thirty others ran to the other side. He carried his book bag in one hand and his trumpet case in the other. He didn't have much homework that night, so he knew that he would have time to change clothes and join the others at the fort before dinnertime.

As he rounded the corner of his street, a police cruiser slowly made its way out of the cul de sac, followed by a red and white ambulance with the letters E.M.S. emblazoned on its side. Neighbors, mostly women, were gathered in small groups by the curbside outside Ned's house. On the porch, sitting in one of the white rockers was his mother, head in hands. Jeff's mom, from across the street, knelt in front of her with her hands on Anita's knees.

Death and taxes! The Right Reverend John Henry Reed, husband, father, man of God, had died suddenly right there at the dining room table while signing his FORM 1040.

****

The funeral was on Saturday, delayed an extra day by the mandatory autopsy required by the Medical Examiner. Preliminary results indicated that John Reed had experienced a massive coronary. The report would eventually include a litany of medical terms, but the coroner could just as well have summarized John's death with the words, "he didn't know what hit him."

There was a bit of family tension amid the final preparations. John had made it clear that he wanted to be cremated. It was not a common practice in the seventies, and theologically troublesome to many. One evening months before while doing homework at the kitchen table, Ned overheard a rather heated discussion between his father and Grandpa Reed.

"It's just not right, son, burning up your body that way. What's going to happen at the Resurrection?"

John Reed replied, "Dad, I'll let God worry about that. He made the first body out of nothing. He'll just have to make a new one."

Ned's father would probably have been uncomfortable at his own funeral service. He was what might be called a "low-church" kind of man. But the Diocese never said farewell to one of its own without all the liturgical bells and whistles. The aroma of incense would permeate the church for months to come. Ned sat quietly as the Bishop waxed eloquently about his dear friend, Father John Reed. As he listened he wondered if the Bishop really knew his dad personally.

It was all overwhelming for a ten year-old. The adults were grieving in their own ways. Anita Reed graciously accepted the condolences of hundreds of parishioners, public officials and friends. Ned's normally animated mother seemed to be robotic in her gestures and facial expressions. Brian was striking in his dress uniform. The military had performed a minor miracle in whisking him half-way around the world in the space of three days. The Air Force transport wasn't exactly the Concorde, but he arrived home in plenty of time. Brian held that impressive military bearing. He seemed to be enjoying the attention of the other mourners. Each visit home his brother seemed more and more a stranger to Ned.

Kara was a bundle of nervous energy. She took it upon herself to see to any last minute details, though there weren't really any. The only image that came to mind for Ned as he watched his sister flit about the room, was that of the Mad Hatter from "Alice in Wonderland." She too was much too preoccupied to notice a brave but frightened little boy who suddenly felt emotionally isolated from all those who had been the bedrock of his existence.

Ned Francis Reed made a decision that day. He would have to rely solely on himself to make his way in the world. It was a misguided insight that cut short his childhood, and would leave him with issues of trust, intimacy and personal ambition that would dominate the landscape of his life.

****

The weeks following Reverend John Henry's untimely death were chaotic. Unknown to Ned, what had been the Reed *home* for twenty-three years was not the Reed *house*. The parish had for generations provided a parsonage for its priest and his family. As gracious, loving and supportive as the church had been in the wake of their loss, the reality was that the Reeds now had to find their own place to live.

Money was an issue from the start. Unfortunately, John was not a big believer in life insurance. He had one policy, the proceeds of which Anita wisely put aside. She was determined to provide a way for her youngest child to attend college, should he desire to do so. She also went back to work full-time, on the 7-3 shift at St. Vincent's.

Before returning to duty Brian shared with his mother that he had been invited by the Marines to enter OCS – Officer Candidate School. He had chosen to make the military his life career. The same evening over dinner Kara revealed that her two closest friends approached her about sharing a three-bedroom apartment near the ferry. Reluctantly she gave her daughter her blessing.

And so it was to be just the two of them for the next eight years. Ned's mother found a small two-bedroom apartment on the second floor of a house not far from the old neighborhood, but still within the same school district. Ned saw his old friends only at school. He was invited back for a birthday party or two the first year.

There was never another mention of the fort again.

• •

During the days of the wake and funeral and in the weeks following, many well-intentioned people reminded Ned that he was now the man of the family. He didn't know exactly what that meant, but he sensed that he was being given a big responsibility. He became hyper-sensitive to his mother's moods and tried not to burden her with his own need to be nurtured. She was having enough problems, he reasoned, so the least he could do was fend for himself. Anita loved him, but construed his independence as a sign that he was getting along fine.

Ned made some friendships in the new neighborhood, but they weren't like the old ones. Most days he would get home an hour or so before his mother and go right to his room. Occasionally he would play some "stick-ball" in the street with neighborhood kids. But he was no longer a leader. He would stand around and wait to be picked for a team.

During breaks in the school year, Ned would spend most days with his father's parents. They were very attentive. They would often play board games with him, and he knew that there would always be a plate of freshly-baked cookies handy. His grandfather also taught him to use the tools in his elaborate wood shop.

Ned's other grandparents, Walter and Elizabeth (Betty) Randolph lived in a sprawling lake house on Lake Hopatcong in New Jersey. He spent his summers there, and his mom spent much time there also, often commuting to her job in Staten Island.

Walter Randolph was a college professor at Rutgers University. He spent most of the summer reading and preparing for his fall courses. His wife, like her daughter, was wiry and energetic, always on the move. So Ned spent a lot of time alone at the lake. There was plenty to do and explore. He had a small rowboat that served as his own personal pirate ship, fishing boat or cruise liner. He had an active imagination so he was never bored.

This was the pattern for Anita and Ned Reed for years ten through fourteen of his life. They still attended church every Sunday except on the one weekend a month when Anita had to work. His father had given him his first communion just three weeks before his death. For young Ned faith was never a religion, but a relationship with God. In the confusion and pain following his father's death, he found it a comfort. He remembered reading about how Jesus cried when he lost a friend, and he imagined how sad God must have felt the day John Reed's heart stopped beating. For this sensitive ten year-old God was not a puppeteer pulling the strings of human marionettes, but a loving coach overseeing the game of life. He would embrace this conviction for the rest of his life.

CHAPTER THREE

They were sitting targets on the sidewalk. Ned pulled her into the doorway of a closed bakery. Examining her arm he found that she had only been grazed by the assassin's bullet. The bleeding was already subsiding. He took a handkerchief from his pocket and tied it around her bicep. She leaned against the store window from which the proprietor had removed all the leftover goods of the day. Though dazed, she was gradually realizing that Ned was not a foe but a friend.

"Where are you staying? Are you alone? Is there anyone I can contact?"

Ned was trying to formulate a plan. All she could do was shake her head from side to side. Knowing that they had to move, he led her into an alley and out the other side on a back street. Crossing between two houses, he half-pulled, half-carried her on to a path that led up the hillside to his place. In less than ten minutes the two of them sat gasping for breath in his living room. Neither could speak, nor felt the need to do so.

Finally, Ned rose and went into the bathroom. After throwing some cold water in his face, he removed some items from the medicine cabinet and returned to the main room. His guest was right where he left her. Without a word he opened a bottle of hydrogen peroxide and dabbed her wound with a cotton swab. She flinched from the sting as the healing balm did its work. Ned then overlapped a couple of band-aids to cover the spot.

As he raised his head their eyes met, and they gazed at one another for several seconds. In that glance he saw confusion and fear. She saw kindness, concern and strength.

Breaking the spell, Ned spoke. "I suppose this would be a good time to introduce ourselves."

That seemed to release the tension and brought a weak smile to her face.

"Yes, it would be nice to know the name of the man who saved my life. My name is Jill Hovnanian."

"And mine is John Henry," he said.

"Well, John Henry, thank you for what you did for me tonight. If you could just tell me how to get back to the port, I'll be on my way."

"Whoah there! First, someone tried to kill you less than an hour ago. Second, if you could find the harbor there are no boats leaving the island until morning. Third, what will you tell those who ask why you are wearing a bloody dress? Fourth, your friend with the gun is still on this very small island. And finally, I am now involved in this thing, and I want to know why. The police will be looking for you *and* for me after what happened at Pablo's. Why don't you want them involved, and what can be so bad that there is no one who can help you? And if those aren't enough questions, I'll think of a few more."

Ned could see the blood drain from Jill's face as she absorbed what he said. She pressed back into the cushions of the sofa as tears began to roll down her cheeks. He moved over next to her and she put her head on his shoulder. She felt safe with this man.

"Are you sure you want to know the answers to your questions?" she whispered.

"Yes, I do Jill Hovnanian. But first I want to make a phone call. I would rather that we contact the police ourselves than have them knock on my door later. Trust me on this. They need to know that you were the victim tonight. Maybe we can meet them in the morning and you can give them a statement."

"I don't know."

"Listen, whatever you tell them beyond what's happened tonight is up to you."

She raised her hands in surrender. "I'm sorry, I've been only thinking about myself, John. I don't want to get you into any trouble. So make the call. Then we'll talk."

CHAPTER FOUR

U neventful is not the word that would describe Ned Reed's fifteenth year. Graduation from P.S. 30 brought an end to nine years, including kindergarten, of his experience in that relatively protective environment. His circle of friends remained small. At the beginning of July he joined his grandparents at the lake. During the previous term Walter Randolph had suffered a severe heart attack while teaching a class at Rutgers. His recovery was slow, so many of the household chores fell to Ned. In all the years he had frolicked at the lake, he had never lifted a finger.

That summer Ned's beloved New York Yankees, led by slugger Reggie Jackson, were beating up on all the competition. His listened to every game on a pocket-sized transistor radio he had received as a graduation gift.

The day after Labor Day he boarded the #6 Bus to start his freshman year at Port Richmond High School. He had never had a problem with academics, but otherwise his life seemed to take another step backwards. The graduation ceremony from grade school was the last time he touched his trumpet, where he played verse after verse of "Pomp and Circumstance," as most of the other eighth graders marched into the auditorium in their blue gowns. Though an avid sports fan, he had no interest in participating in sports activities or to even attend any games. Within the first week of high school he established his routine of leaving at the close of the day, and walking to the bus stop to reboard the bus without speaking to a single soul.

One Friday, after the Christmas holidays, Anita Reed got home from work a little early. She knocked on her son's bedroom door and slowly entered. Ned was finishing what little homework he had been assigned for the weekend.

"How's my favorite man?" she said, as she sat on the edge of the bed. "We haven't had much time together lately. How about we go out and grab a pepperoni pizza at Joe and Pat's?" It was Ned's favorite place to eat.

Anita and Ned found a table in the corner where they would have a clear view of Tony, whose tossing of pizza dough was legendary. As they sipped on Cokes while their dinner was baking, Anita asked her son everything about school. Her attentiveness, for some reason, made him feel uncomfortable. As he began his meal his mother continued to look at him.

"Ned," she finally said, "You know that you are the most important person in my life?"

All he could do was nod. Something was obviously coming that he wasn't sure he wanted to hear.

She continued. "I loved your dad more than anything. I thought that we would grow old together. I still miss him."

Here it comes.

"I've been feeling a kind of loneliness that I don't suppose you'll fully understand until you're grown and on your own. There is a wonderful man that I've met at work. We have been having lunch together for a few months. He lost his wife to cancer five years ago. We have decided to see each other outside the hospital. What do you think?"

Ned looked into his mother's eyes but couldn't utter a word.

She rambled on. "Honey, you're not going to believe this, but do you know what he does at the hospital? He's a chaplain. He's a minister, Ned, just like your dad. He has two children that are about Kara's age. I've been wanting to tell you about this for a while…..Sweetheart, tell me what you're feeling?"

He was no longer hungry or thirsty. They ate quietly. When they left the restaurant, Anita slipped her hand through his arm. She would say no more until he was ready.

• •

Anita and Bill Campbell dated through Spring and Summer of '78. He, a Lutheran, began attending church with her and Ned almost every Sunday. Ned was surprised that Bill seemed to know all the responses in the liturgy in the Episcopal Church. Each week after services they would grab a bite to eat somewhere. Frequently they would take a ride to New Jersey, exploring some of the quaint towns along the coast.

It became apparent to Ned that his mother was limited in her taste for men. Bill Campbell and John Reed were amazingly alike, even in some of their mannerisms. It stirred mixed feelings in him. At times Bill seemed to invade that special place he held just for his dad. At other times the similarities in this man he found comforting.

The week before school resumed that year, Ned found himself alone with Bill in his backyard. Anita seemed to have disappeared all of a sudden. He sensed a set-up.

Bill turned to him. "Ned, I guess you can see how much I care about your mom. Well, I'm going to ask her to marry me. I'm not sure how you feel about that, but I hope you can accept me into your life. I will never try to take your father's place."

Ned was prepared for this moment. He liked Bill. He saw the happiness that he brought to his mother. He wanted to tell him that he missed having a dad, and that Bill was welcome. But there was a gnawing fear that held him back. He didn't want to ever be in the position of losing another significant man in his life. When he opened his mouth the only words that came out were, "Would I have to change my name?"

CHAPTER FIVE

Ned made a call to Pablo's. The owner answered on the first ring.

"Pablo, this is John Henry. Have the police arrived?"

"*Si, Senor* Henry, they are questioning everyone. This is not so good for business. Where did you go?"

"I'll explain later, Pablo. Is Chief Rivera there by any chance? I need to speak with him."

Juan Rivera had been a New York City Policeman. After putting in his twenty years, he retired at the rank of Lieutenant. He saw an ad in the New York Times for the position of Police Chief on San Marcos Island. With their children already in college, he and his wife thought it might be an adventure worth pursuing. Both from Puerto Rican families, they were also bi-lingual from the cradle.

They flew down to the islands, and boated to San Marcos at their own expense. Sailing into East Harbor, they knew they were home. Juan's interview with the Island Council went very well and they offered him the job on the spot. The salary was low by U.S. standards, but with his pension and the lower cost of living, they looked forward to a comfortable life.

John Henry had crossed paths with Rivera on several occasions. The longest conversation they had lasted barely ten minutes. The lawman happened upon him on a lonely stretch of the Belt one day. Ned was trying to repair a flat tire on his ten-speed. Rivera offered him a ride home. Noting his New York speech inflections, the Chief showed a friendly curiosity about his presence on the island. It was an uncomfortable ride for Ned. He tried to keep the conversation light and away from himself. But he sensed that he was only intensifying the policeman's interest.

It was a few minutes before Rivera finally came to the phone.

"Mr. Henry," he said, "it seems that you're missing our little party here. I am told that you and a young lady left in a bit of a hurry. May I ask where you are?"

"That's why I'm calling," Ned replied. "The woman was apparently the intended victim, and in the commotion left the cantina in a panic. I managed to catch up with her and brought her to my apartment for safety. She and I would like to cooperate in any way with your investigation. Would it be possible for us to come by the station first thing in the morning?"

"I'd rather not wait," said the Chief. "I understand your concern for her safety, but whoever was responsible for this is no doubt still on the island. I don't think this should wait."

He paused. "I'll tell you what we can do. When I'm finished here I'll just stop by your place. Miss Hov...."

"It's Hovnanian. Yes, she may know more than any of us why this happened. How did you know her name, Chief?"

"She left without her purse. She is also from New York, Mr. Henry. It seems that all of us bring our secrets with us to San Marcos, yes? At any rate, I'll see you in an hour or so."

Rivera's remark unnerved Ned a bit. He had also desired some time alone with his guest to learn more about who might want to bring her harm. Putting the phone down, he returned from the kitchen to the living room and found her sitting in an overstuffed chair with her eyes closed. Hearing him, she looked up with anticipation.

34

"It's OK, Jill. May I call you Jill? The police will come by here a little later. Oh, and they have your purse."

"I don't know what to tell them, John. May I call *you* John? My life is very complicated right now, and I don't see what anyone here can do to change it."

"I told you that whatever you tell the police is up to you. But I remind you that you're still in danger, and this is a very tiny island. After Chief Rivera is done with us, I am going to have some questions too. Will you let me ask them?"

"I guess I owe you that much. By the way, what is it you do here? From what I saw earlier, you took control of the situation like you knew what you were doing. I thought maybe you were a cop."

"We can talk about me later," Ned replied. "Right now I suggest you get out of that dress into something that won't get blood all over my furniture. I can't help you in the underwear department, but I do have some things that might fit you."

"Thank you. I'm sorry that you've gotten caught up in my troubles. You've done enough for me already." Then looking at her dress, she smiled. "I think I will accept your offer."

"Good. And expect to stay the night. You can use my bedroom, I'll take the couch. The sheets are clean and you can find towels in the bathroom."

Ten minutes later Jill appeared, clad in red spandex biking pants and a George Washington University sweatshirt that extended down to her knees. She posed momentarily in the doorway. "Not exactly Versace," she said. "But it will do."

CHAPTER SIX

Near the end of his freshman year he found Sharon. They met by accident – literally. She, a sophomore, was late leaving a class and Ned was late arriving for a class in the same room. She burst through the door just as he was rounding a line of lockers. They collided, butting heads and then going down in a heap. A few minutes later they were sitting on opposite chairs in the nurse's office. She had a bloody nose and he a swollen right eye.

"I'm so sorry," Sharon said. "I wasn't looking where I was going."

"No, I was the one who wasn't thinking," he replied.

Ned couldn't take his eyes off of her. It was not the bloody nose, but her beautiful blue eyes. Her blonde hair was cut short and was naturally curly. With her high cheek bones and rosy complexion, she looked like a fashion model. She was slim, but not skinny.

He was a normal fifteen year-old boy. He knew all about sex. When he was eleven his mother, always the nurse, explained things to him. She also gave him a little handbook for easy reference. It was written in such a way as to portray sex as a gift from God to be treasured, not to be arbitrarily given or taken away. He understood all the mechanics. It was the deep feelings he didn't understand…until now.

Ned had virtually no one-to-one experience relating to girls. He had been attracted to several but never had the courage to approach them. The closest he got was when he and Linda Welner were assigned to a science project together. Unfortunately, she was all business. Instinctively Ned knew that Sharon was different. He felt at ease in her presence. He wanted to know her, to know all about her.

"By the way, I'm Ned Reed," he said. "I think I've seen you around the school before. Are you going to be OK?"

She put out her hand. "Sharon Johanson. I can't say that I remember seeing you before today. Anyway, this isn't my first bloody nose, and probably not the last. I'll survive."

They both chuckled and moved into a comfortable flow of conversation. It being the last class period of the day, the nurse suggested they just wait until the bell and leave school from there.

Ned missed the #6 Bus for home that day. He and Sharon walked up to Richmond Avenue and had a slice of pizza at Angelina's. He never imagined that he could have so much in common with a girl. When they finally went their separate ways, Ned turned and watched her until she was out of sight. He was in love.

• •

Sharon and Ned dated for two years. Since you had to be eighteen to have a driver's license in New York, they had to use public transportation to get anywhere. Sometimes they would ride the ferry over to Manhattan and back again. The view of the skyline and of the Statue of Liberty was awesome at night. On the return trip they had a special place to sit, sheltered from the wind. The World Trade Center and

Empire State Building dwarfed the rest of the city, with their lighted antennas reaching into the heavens.

They walked all over the Island. Often they would be silent for periods of time, yet they were never at a loss for words. Sharon was a great listener, and Ned shared things with her that he had never said to anyone, including a lot of memories of his dad. He wanted to talk to her about these things.

About a month after their initial encounter they shared their first kiss. He had walked her home from Westerleigh Park. While saying goodbye they leaned toward one another at the same time. It was an electric moment. Neither said anything after it. They just smiled at each other and she ran into the house.

Ned knew that many of his classmates were sexually active. He wondered if he was retarded in this area. He felt great desire for Sharon. Sometimes he imagined what it would be like to make love to her. He wondered if she had expectations of him that he was not fulfilling.

One evening while watching TV at her house they shared a deep and passionate kiss. They held each other tightly for a time. There was an awkwardness between them that he hadn't known before. Then she looked up at him and said, "Ned we have to talk."

That was how they parted that night. He was awake well into the night wondering, no fearing, what the *talk* would be about. After school the next day, they walked up to Angelina's and found a booth in the back. As they sipped their sodas Sharon initiated the conversation.

"Ned, you are a great guy and I love you, I do. But you have to know something about me. On my wedding day I plan to be a virgin. I don't care what other people do or say. I look forward to the first time, but I'm going to wait. Do you understand what I'm trying to say?"

He didn't know whether to be disappointed or relieved. Sharon was drawing a line in the sand in their relationship which he could not cross. At that moment he realized that he would not have taken the initiative to cross that line with her. The two of them had developed first an emotional and spiritual bond that was more important to him now than sexual intercourse ever could be. So he thought, if she could wait, so could he. And that's just what he told her over a pepperoni pizza at Angelina's, in his sixteenth year.

CHAPTER SEVEN

Juan Rivera was a man of his word. In an hour he was knocking on Ned's door. In the meantime the two of them had rediscovered their appetites and shared a light snack of cheese, veggies and crackers. Ned found also a bottle of Sangria in the refrigerator. They were just cleaning up when Rivera arrived.

Ned could not suppress a smile when the policeman appeared in the doorway. The man had obviously transformed himself from N.Y.P.D. cop to tropical lawman. He wore a light tan linen suit with a colorful shirt opened at the collar. In his left hand he held a panama hat with a teal blue band. He had also grown a thin mustache since the last time Ned had seen him.

"Chief, thank you for coming. I see you remembered where I lived."

"It's a small island, Mr. Henry. I'm getting to know where everyone lives."

Ned introduced Jill and the three of them found comfortable chairs. He noticed that Rivera's eyes were subtly evaluating the environment. He knew the look. He himself had done it thousands of times. Rivera took out a small notebook and set about his work.

"I didn't learn much from my interviews at the cantina. This apparently happened so quickly no one remembers anything. From what I gather, the two of you are my prime witnesses. So Mr. Henry, I'd like to hear from you first."

Ned carefully described the scene, from his sighting of the barrel of the gun, his instinctive lunge, the scuffle, Jill's hasty exit, and his efforts to take her out of harm's way. The struggle with the gunman lasted only a few seconds. All Ned could recollect was that he was a stocky man with dark hair. There was a second man waiting on a red Vespa scooter, and they were gone from sight almost immediately.

Chief Rivera had a few follow-up questions but they yielded no further information. He then turned to face Jill.

"OK, Miss Hovnanian, it's your turn."

"It's *Mrs.* Hovnanian..." In saying this she glanced at Ned and they held eye contact for a moment.

"All right, Mrs. Hovnanian. When you arrived here on San Marcos earlier today you indicated that you came as a tourist. Could you elaborate on that for me? Why did you come to *our* island?"

"I needed to get away for a while. Before I married, I worked for a travel agency. I remembered reading an article in a trade magazine titled, 'Hidden Gem in the Caribbean.' It was all about this place. I guess I thought it would be a nice place to vacation."

Rivera wrinkled his brow. "You came alone. This is unusual. What about your husband?"

Jill answered quickly. "My husband is a very busy man who is away from home for extended periods of time. I decided to take this trip on a whim. It was too late for any of my friends to change their plans."

The policeman let her response hang in the air for a moment. It was as if he expected her to say more. Finally, he moved on. "We all seem to agree that you were the target of this attack. But why? Why you, Mrs. Hovnanian?"

"I have no idea!"

"Is there anyone who would have reason to do you harm?"

"No," she said. "It makes no sense."

"Did you notice anything suspicious on your journey here? For instance, was there anyone who was on your flight from Barbados *and* on the boat to San Marcos?"

"I can't help you there. I was reading most of the time. I spoke to no one, and wasn't noticing anyone in particular."

Continued questioning yielded similar results. Eventually, Rivera ran out of questions. Finally he shrugged.

"How long had you planned to stay on San Marcos, madam?"

"I was to be here a week, but now…"

"I must ask you to remain until we have dealt fully with this matter. Tomorrow we will speak further, and I will arrange for protection of you. You should be safe here tonight."

Before leaving, the Chief turned once more and looked at Jill. "Is there anything else you haven't told me?" She just shook her head.

Ned had observed closely as Rivera questioned Jill. He was hoping to learn more himself about this woman who was now his surprise house guest. He realized that he didn't know much more than he did before. He also picked up the same vibes as the policeman. He wondered if she would be open with him.

After the door closed behind Rivera, Ned turned to her. "My turn, Jill. That was part of our agreement."

She excused herself to use the bathroom. When she returned she announced, "I know we need to talk, John. But I am totally exhausted. Let me get some rest and I promise we can talk for as long as you want in the morning."

She didn't wait for an answer. "Good night," she said, and closed the bedroom door behind her.

· ·

It was almost midnight before Ned fell into a deep sleep. The couch was uncomfortable, but not as uncomfortable as the thoughts running through his mind. Somehow he knew that his days on San Marcos were now numbered. He had made many transitions in his life, but they were all planned. This one was not.

He had been an active dreamer since childhood. His dreams were often quite detailed. As a psychology major in college, he did an extensive study of dream analysis and interpretation. He became proficient at analyzing the dreams of dorm mates and other friends. But when it came to his own dreaming, Ned remained a mystery to himself. His dreams almost always carried similar themes: danger, God, curiosity, and falling – but not necessarily in that order. He was thankful that in none of his dreams thus far had he ever hit bottom.

On this night Ned Reed found himself in a primitive environment. He was alone, as usual, but still felt that many eyes were watching his every move. Out of the shadows he heard a rhythmic sound, like that of a distant drum. As he walked the path, the sound grew in intensity. It became louder and louder until his ears were hurting. He covered them and began to run.

Ahead of him was a bank of clouds that had settled close to the forest floor. He threw himself into the dense fog. He could not see and felt intense heat. His eyes began to water, and he took a huge breath which caused him to cough violently.

Ned rolled off the couch and opened his eyes. He was still coughing. He was perspiring and he could not see. The living room was filled with thick smoke. He was suddenly fully awake. Remaining on the floor he began to crawl, arm over arm toward the bedroom door. He reached up, turned the knob, pushed it open, and called Jill's name. There was no response. He made his way across to the bed and pulled her down beside him. She too awakened in a coughing fit.

He guided her until they reached the sliding door leading to the balcony. Pulling it open, he shoved her out and the two of them stood at the railing and breathed in large gulps of night air. Smoke billowed through the open door and they could feel intense heat from below.

"Wait here," Ned shouted. "I'll be right back."

Crouching low and inhaling deeply he reentered the room, pulled open the closet and kicked out a false panel behind his shoes. He grabbed a small duffel bag and made it out to the balcony just as his lungs were about to burst.

Jill was frozen in fear. Smoke was now everywhere. Ned took her by the shoulders and shook her.

"We are going to jump together. Trust me, we'll be OK."

He threw the bag over the side, helped her into a sitting position on the railing, and then joined her.

"On the count of three, take a deep breath, push off and jump. One, two, three!"

The heat of the fire gave way to a rush of cool, chlorinated water. They went to the bottom of the complex's swimming pool and immediately bobbed to the surface. They moved to the shallow end and lay momentarily on the apron of the pool. Ned then got to his feet and extended his hand to Jill.

"We've got to get out of here," he said. "Come on!"

With that he retrieved the duffel from the grass nearby and they took off the same way they had come several hours before. He led her through the quiet streets down to a marina by the harbor. They saw no one on the way. On a quay with a few dozen boat slips, Ned lifted her aboard a thirty foot Boston Whaler. There was an explosion behind them and they turned and looked up as pillars of fire shot through the roof of his building on the hillside.

Ned fired up the engines, unhooked the lines, and backed the boat out of the slip. Slowly he moved out toward the mouth of the harbor in complete darkness. He didn't dare turn on any lights.

When they reached open water, he set the autopilot on a course to the west and joined Jill in the cabin. There she sat shivering, still in her spandex and sweatshirt.

He smiled. "Welcome aboard, M'lady. It looks like you could use another change of clothes."

"How? What? This boat?"…..

"Relax. It's mine."

She looked around. Hanging on the wall a small life preserver bore the name of the boat. "Death and Taxes?" she said.

"It's a long story, Jill."

CHAPTER EIGHT

On the first of April, 1980 Sharon Johanson received an acceptance letter from the University of Minnesota. She had applied to several local colleges, but U. of M was always her first choice. It was a sensitive subject with Ned who, as a junior, would be left behind physically and emotionally when Sharon moved on to Minnesota. She tried to reassure him, promising to write all the time and call at least once a week.

What neither of them knew was that her parents had already decided to return to Minnesota themselves after her graduation from high school. Her father requested a transfer back to the home office in the Twin Cities. There would be no holiday or summer times in Staten Island. Their relationship would be put to the ultimate test.

For two years Ned had enjoyed a season of relative serenity. Sharon was his soul-mate. She drew him into new activities and interests. She was his first, and he assumed his only love. That night the two of them planned to go to a movie. She had called him at home the moment she opened the letter. But at the dinner table that evening her parents told her of their plans to return to the Midwest. They were surprised by her emotional reaction.

She was quieter than usual on the way to the theater. Afterward they walked slowly toward home. This time it was Ned who broke the ice.

"What's wrong Sharon? I thought this would be a happy day for you. You got accepted to Minnesota. We'll see each other a lot. The time will go fast."

Then, with tears in her eyes, she told him the rest of the news.

"They can't do that! Don't they know? Don't they understand about us?"

"Ned, it's a done deal. The middle of August my family is moving to Minneapolis."

The rest of the way home they did their own versions of damage control. Promises were made. Trips were planned. Nothing would keep them apart. But a strange thing happened after that night. Without ever discussing it, the two of them entered into a pact of denial. For the next four months they treated that April Fools' Day as if it was a bad joke. In June Ned received his long-awaited driver's license. He was given a second-hand VW Beetle by the Randolphs. He washed and vacuumed it twice a week.

They used the Beetle to go to Sharon's senior prom. It was held at the Staaten, the Island's premier restaurant and catering hall. Most of the other students arrived in Cadillacs and Lincoln limousines. The valet parking attendant gave Ned a wink as he drove away in the bug.

That summer Ned took a part-time job doling out soft ice-cream cones at the South Beach Amusement Park. He made just enough money to pay his car expenses and to take Sharon places. They spent a lot of time at the beach.

The night before the big move, Sharon and Ned rode the ferry one last time. It was a bittersweet voyage for both of them. Later they drove to the beach and spread out a large beach towel. The sun had set and the only light was cast by the moon in the eastern sky.

Words weren't necessary that night. They clung to one another and kissed. Their desire for each other was stronger at that moment than ever before. She held his face in her hands. "I love you, Ned Reed. And someday, someday...."

• •

The love that would last forever could not survive one semester. Initially they wrote daily, and spoke to one another every Monday night. By the time he started the school year she had been in class already for three weeks. Her letters were filled with excitement, reflecting a freedom she had never known before. She was meeting new friends, and sororities were approaching her about rushing.

In stark contrast, Ned began school in a somber mood. There was little that evoked excitement. He realized just how great a void Sharon had filled in him during their time together, and now how empty he was again.

By October the letters became more infrequent. As their worlds grew further apart there was less to share. Their weekly conversations became awkward. It was painful for both of them. The Sunday after Thanksgiving Ned was watching a football game when the phone rang. His mother called to him from the kitchen. It was Sharon.

"Is everything all right?" he said as soon as he took the phone.

"No," she replied, in little more than a whisper. "Ned, I couldn't wait another day. I've been thinking a lot about us. I don't want to hurt you, but things have changed between us since August. I think you know it too."

As at many other poignant moments in his young life he found himself speechless. He just could not say what he was feeling. He wanted to tell her that he sensed this time was coming. To tell her how miserable he was without her. That he felt her slipping away. But he could not say a word.

"Ned, are you still there. Talk to me."

"I'm here. Is it another guy?" he blurted out.

"Is that what you think? The answer is no," she said with a note of agitation. I just think that we have found that it isn't the same for us, being together and being apart. I believe we should stop writing for now."

"And calling?"

"Yes, and calling too. I never thought that this could happen. I'm sorry if I've let you down. I just don't know what else to do."

"Me either."

There was little else to say. These two who would talk for hours on end had run out of words. The conversation, their last, ended with sorrowful good-byes. When he hung up, Ned quietly retreated to his room. It no longer mattered who was winning the football game, or even what he would be doing the next day. He recognized the emptiness.

That's what happens when you love someone too much. You lose them. It's not worth the risk.

In frustration he pushed a stack of books off his desk onto the floor. On top of the pile lay one book which had opened randomly to a particular page. It was his Bible. He snatched it up and read these words which he had underlined at an earlier time: "We know that all things work together for good for them that love God."

"It better be true, God. I'm going to hold you to it!"

CHAPTER NINE

Jill fell fast asleep in a terrycloth robe that Ned took from a fully stocked closet in the cabin of the boat. He returned to the main deck and opened the duffel bag that he had hastily stowed under one of the seats. He surveyed its contents. There were several packs of U.S. currency, at least a dozen passports bearing a variety of names, a brown leather make-up kit, some clothes, and a nine millimeter glock pistol on top of several boxes of ammunition. In addition, he fished out a small notebook filled with a series of numbers which corresponded with bank accounts in Zurich, Switzerland and the Cayman Islands. An identical book was kept in a safe-deposit box at a branch of Richmond County Savings Bank in New York.

By mid-morning Ned guided the boat into a marina on the southern tip of Barbados. A small gratuity to the marina's owner bypassed the need for any paperwork. With his valuables safely locked in a hidden compartment, the two of them took a taxi to Bridgetown, the principal business district on the island. The first stop was to replace Jill's unusual wardrobe with some proper attire. Within a half-hour she emerged from a shop in shorts, tank top and beach shoes. She carried shopping bags on either arm.

Next he had Jill check into a small tourist hotel, the Tropicana. From there they followed directions to the United States Consulate Office. The plan was for her to report that her purse was missing, which it was, and that she needed documentation so that she could return home.

It went very smoothly. Apparently she was one of many tourists who had had the same story in a matter of days. After verifying her information, she was told to see the local authorities about the missing purse, and then to stop back later in the day for her paperwork. It helped that the flight on which she arrived was to Barbados, and that the airline was able to confirm her travel information.

Walking out into the mid-day sun they found their way to an outdoor café with round tables sheltered by pastel-colored umbrellas. After ordering drinks, Ned fixed his gaze on Jill.

"It's time, *Mrs.* Hovnanian, that you tell me what's going on. I want to know it all. We can sit here all afternoon if necessary. As you said yourself, you owe me that much. After that we can see what we can do about contacting your husband and getting you on a flight to New York."

"It's not that simple. I can't go home. It's very possible that my husband is involved in what happened in San Marcos."

"Slow down," he said. "Let's start at the beginning."

****

It was almost four o'clock when they left the café. In less than twenty-four hours Ned Reed's life had taken a U-Turn. John Henry no longer existed. And if what Jill shared with him was true, and he believed it was, he would not abandon her here. Whatever the future would bring it would have to wait until this new mission was done. And he wondered inwardly if this beautiful young woman might somehow be a part of that future.

There were no evening flights available back to the States. At the travel desk in the Tropicana they made arrangements to fly the next morning to New York, with one stop in Miami. Jill had no cash or credit cards. She agreed that she would not attempt to have the cards replaced. Ned suspected that her travel and purchases were somehow being monitored and that this might put her pursuers back on her trail. He paid for everything in cash.

There was a Chinese take-out down the block from the hotel. They bought sweet and sour pork, egg drop soup, and a couple of shrimp rolls to bring back to the room. He chose to use chop sticks, she the plastic tableware. Noting his adept use of the sticks she said, "You are a man of many talents, John. Or should I now call you Richard. You should have warned me when the embassy person asked to see your passport. So who are you, Richard Carlson?"

"At this point the less you know about me the better, Jill. Let's just say that in my profession it has been necessary to go by different names at different times."

She shook her head. "I feel like I've given you my life story today, but I don't even know your real name."

"All you need to know is that I will help you get off someone's hit list. From what you've told me, we have to start in New York. You'll just have to trust me."

They ate quietly for a time. She looked at him intently. "Twice you've saved my life. I *do* trust you!"

"Then you can call me Ned."

The hotel room was spacious but had just one king-size bed. Ned did not offer to sleep on the floor, and she didn't ask him to. There was a growing tension as they took turns in the bathroom and finally settled on opposite sides of the bed. She wore a nightshirt she had bought earlier in the day, and he wore his undershirt and boxers.

First she began to giggle and then he joined her. They had now been together only a little more than thirty hours, and here they were like an old married couple tucked in for the night. All the intensity of their flight from danger drained away in that moment, and they were overtaken by exhaustion.

"Good night, Jill."

"Good night 'John-boy', or whoever you are."

Ned dreamed again that night. But for the first time in many years he didn't dream about fear, or danger, or falling. He was on a beach on a beautiful moon-lit night.....with a pretty girl.

Ned awoke to sounds of the city a little after seven am. He opened his eyes and found himself in the middle of the bed with Jill tucked in the crook of his arm. Her eyes were wide open and she had a warm smile on her face.

"How did you get over here?" he asked.

"I was just about to ask you the same question. A girl could get the wrong idea under these circumstances."

He gave her a playful squeeze and then made his way to the shower. She watched him until he disappeared. *What a strange man. I've never met anyone like him. Is he playing hard to get? No, I don't think that's it.* All that she knew so far was that he was kind, decisive and secretive. And in regard to her, a gentleman.

By nine they were in a cab heading back to the marina. With the meter still running, Ned collected his documents and some clothes, packing them in a specially designed suitcase he kept on board. He gave Jill his duffel for her belongings. After paying dock fees in advance, he closed up the Whaler and they set off for the airport in the nearby town of St. Philip.

As the 737 banked to the north after take-off, Jill squeezed his hand.

"Whatever happens now, I want you to know that I won't forget what you've done."

Eyes closed and deep in thought, he seemed not to hear her. But when she tried to withdraw her hand, he didn't let go.

CHAPTER TEN

If it's possible to have a taste of hell on earth, Ned's last year of high school might have qualified. He spiraled down into a deep depression. He was already 6'2", but his weight dropped by fifteen pounds. He was lethargic and moody. He would disappear for hours on end. School was his only diversion, and amazingly his grades did not suffer.

Anita and Bill took him first to the pastor of their church, and then at his recommendation, to a therapist. He was immediately placed on some medication and she began meeting with Ned twice a week. She was a good listener and he was able to open up to her about Sharon, their deep relationship, and the emptiness that followed their break-up.

Ironically, her name was also Sharon, Dr. Sharon Perrone. She was impressed by both the vulnerability and the inner strength of this teenager. Though a skillful counselor, she found him to be a formidable challenge. It was clear that Ned was setting the limits of his therapy. She wanted to talk about his father, Anita, and Bill. He wouldn't go there. She wanted to do some psychological testing, but he wouldn't hear of it. It was as if he consented to come only to cope with the loss of Sharon Johanson. Other issues he would deal with himself. It seemed to her a decision that had long before been set in stone.

After just three months Ned was no longer on medication. He liked Dr. Perrone, but they seemed to have run out of steam. He was feeling much better. He was looking forward to beginning his freshman year at George Washington University in Washington, D.C.. Early in the summer it was he that informed her that her services would no longer be needed.

"Dr. P, I think we've come to the end of the road. You've been a big help to me, but I'm OK now."

The doctor sensed that this moment was coming. She believed there was much more to do for Ned, but he was shutting the door. After trying to negotiate for a few more sessions for closure, she gave up.

"Ned, you are a remarkable young man. I believe you'll accomplish a lot in your lifetime. I want you to understand, however, that the way you have chosen may be a lonely one at times. The door to the human heart opens only from the inside. There will be many others who will seek to enter it. You are a formidable gate-keeper."

Ned was deeply moved by her words. He regarded her not just as a therapist but as a friend. She had walked with him patiently, respecting his boundaries. He would always be grateful to her. As he was preparing to leave the office, he surprised her with a big hug.

"By the way, Doc. You never asked me what I want to major in at GW. With a big smile he pronounced the four-syllable word: "PSY CHOL O GY."

• •

Ned finished fifth academically in his class of 350. Graduation was to be on the athletic field, but the threat of rain forced the back-up plan to use the old Port Richmond movie theater. It had succumbed to the competition of the new multi-plexes years before. But it was saved by placement on the historical register, and restored for special events.

To the surprise of his family and all in attendance, Ned was called to the stage to receive the award as the top math student. With it came a $3,000 college scholarship.

That evening Anita joined her son on the glider on the front porch.

"I'm very proud of you, Ned. After all you've been through, you came out on top. I have one last surprise for you today. When your father died, he left some money so that you could go to college one day. With your scholarship it should be enough. It is his special gift for you."

Tears rolled down his face. After nine years he still missed his dad. He felt bad that on this special day in his life he hadn't thought about him once. Guilt and sorrow finally brought the tears he had long denied.

Ned worked that summer as a "gopher" for a local builder. He had to go for coffee, go for materials and nails at the lumber yard, or anything else that was needed. By August, he had saved enough to replace the VW with a five year-old Camaro, but got to drive it only two weeks before leaving for D.C. Freshman were not allowed cars, and with parking in Washington always at a premium, he figured that during the school year he would need a bicycle.

On August 16th, Bill and Ned worked all morning loading the family van with all his worldly possessions. After lunch the three of them headed across the Outerbridge Crossing and down the New Jersey Turnpike toward the nation's capitol. Because of crowded dorms, he was assigned to a three bedroom apartment just two blocks from campus on G Street. He was the first to arrive. After settling him in, they all ate at a nearby Ponderosa Steakhouse. Early that evening Ned stood on the sidewalk and watched as they drove out of sight.

CHAPTER ELEVEN

It was twilight as the flight from Miami took a northerly approach down the Hudson River en route to Kennedy Airport. The fading sun reflected off the thousands of windows of the Manhattan skyline facing the west. Ned had been preparing himself for a culture shock after his months in paradise, but the sight of the city actually had a calming effect on him. He was coming home again. He was being called back to life again.

Jill had slept most of the way. He spent the time contemplating their next step. They deplaned, and by the time they reached the baggage carousel their luggage was waiting for them.

Soon they were seated in a yellow cab moving toward Manhattan. The driver's command of English was very limited, so Ned decided to sit in the front passenger seat to direct him where they wanted to go. As signs flashed by he was reminded of how New Yorkers abbreviated so many highway and place names. They were on the L.I.E. (Long Island Expressway) heading for the B.Q.E. (Brooklyn-Queens Expressway), on to the "Willy B" (Williamsburg Bridge), across the East River into the "Big Apple."

Their destination was SoHo. Most assumed that it was named for the same section in London. To locals it simply meant, "South of Houston St." (pronounced How-ston).

After a forty minute ride they pulled up in front of a row of quaint, four-family brownstones in Greenwich Village.

As the taxi departed, they stood by the curb and soaked in the sights and the sounds of the neighborhood: a couple walking their Elkhound; a grocer taking in produce from the sidewalk for the night; people in all manner of dress going out or coming home. Ned ushered Jill up the steps of one of the buildings and opened the lobby door. On either side were doors marked A and B. A stairway led up to a second floor which presumably led to C and D.

Ned unlocked B and they stepped into a spacious living area furnished in shades of brown. Angled to the left was a small kitchen with a table and four chairs. Down the hallway from the entry were two bedrooms, each with their own bath. Jill noted that there were live, healthy plants in every room, and lots of impressive art work. What she didn't see was a single photograph.

"Very nice," she commented. "Are you borrowing it from a friend?"

"No, it's mine. The beds are made, the refrigerator is full. Please feel at home."

'But…"

"I have someone who checks on it regularly. I called him from the airport in Miami and asked him to get it ready for us."

"How many homes do you have?"

"Not enough if you keep getting them firebombed. Just joking."

Pointing to the kitchen he said, "We have plenty to eat here, but why don't you freshen up and we can catch a bite nearby. There are some wonderful restaurants all around us."

For late September the evening was mild. They walked through Washington Square Park and found a small bistro with outside tables overlooking the park. Over pasta salads they considered their situation.

Ned asked her, "Now I want you to tell me again the exact words your husband used when he called the other day."

"He said, 'Jill, this is Dave. Don't talk, just listen. Get out of the house, now. You hear me, now! And Jill, I'm sorry, about everything.' And then he just hung up."

"You said he had been missing?"

"I hadn't heard a word in weeks. He was gone a lot, all over the world. But he always called every few days. Not this time. I was actually thinking of contacting the police, but I didn't know where to tell them to look."

"No idea where he was calling from?"

"Ned, he never told me where he was going. It had become an issue in our marriage. I thought I knew him before we married, but David became more distant, and more and more evasive about his work. He was becoming a stranger to me. I think he was into something way over his head."

"Imports-Exports?"

"That's all I ever knew."

Before leaving the bistro he outlined the next day's agenda. "Tomorrow is Sunday," he said. "Sleep in if you can. I have a couple of things to do early, and then I suggest we stop by your place. It's best if we wait until the afternoon when there will be lots of activity in the area. We'll see if your husband has returned. If he has, we'll try to make sense of this. If not, you can gather enough things to keep you for a time. Then I'll pursue some contacts to see where he is or where he's been."

She shivered. "I'm afraid, Ned. I just want to run away from all this."

"You tried that, remember, and it almost got you killed?"

Later that night they watched the eleven o'clock news, and then prepared for bed. He made sure she had everything she needed and then headed for his own room. She turned and called after him, but the door was already closed.

CHAPTER TWELVE

Washington, D.C. was like no where else to live or go to school. Things that drew little attention in the heartland of the country were daily headlines in the Post and the Times. And it seemed that the country or the world was ever on the brink of financial, governmental or diplomatic collapse. The residents of 1600 Pennsylvania, their itineraries, their family members, and even their pets made for daily conversation. The current president was a former movie star who had a way with words. He was making the country feel good about itself again after years of paralyzing inflation and an embarrassing hostage crisis which shook the nation's psyche. His recovery from an assassination attempt just added to his mystique as the country's fearless leader.

Ned thrived in this new environment. He found college to be less rigorous than high school. At Port Richmond he spent seven hours a day in the classroom and most of his evenings doing homework. At GW he only had a few classes a day and lots of time to prepare. He was a quick and disciplined learner.

He liked his freedom and the opportunity to fend for himself. Though not a part of the fraternity scene, he made many friends, both male and female. He dated regularly but preferred to "play the field." Some of his best friends were those he met in the College & Career group at St. Margaret's

Episcopal Church near Dupont Circle, which he faithfully attended.

By his junior year most of Ned's courses were electives in his chosen field of Psychology. It was in an Abnormal Psych course that he met a transfer student from Maryland by the name of Cheryl Blaine. On the first day of class they sat next to one another and he felt an immediate attraction to her. She gave off an aura of self-assurance. She was slight of build, with dark hair and enticing green eyes.

After a week or two of pretending that they didn't notice one another, they found themselves alone before class one day. Apparently it had been cancelled and they were the only two who hadn't gotten the word.

She spoke first. "It looks like we got up early for no reason."

"It appears that way….er…..a……. would you like to get a cup of coffee?"

"Why not?"

They made small talk as they walked to a busy coffee shop around the corner. All the tables were taken, so they sat on stools at the counter. For the second time in his life Ned found himself totally at ease with a woman. But he was no longer a teenager. As if drawn together by some invisible hand, and oblivious to the other patrons, they poured themselves out to one another.

Sometime while sipping his fourth cup of coffee, he looked at Cheryl and said, "I hope this doesn't scare you but I think you're the girl I'm going to marry."

She laughed, but it was neither out of sarcasm nor anxiety. It was more like she had heard a joyful surprise.

She leaned over and kissed him lightly on the lips. "We'll see, Mr. Reed. We'll see."

. . . .

Ned Reed and Cheryl Blaine were married on August 12, 1984, two weeks before their senior years at George Washington University. Both families had tried in vain to convince them to wait until they had received their degrees, but they wouldn't be dissuaded.

The wedding took place at St. Margaret's where Cheryl had also become active during their courtship. Bill Campbell assisted the Rector, Tom Wade, in performing the ceremony. There were less than sixty in attendance, including immediate families, a handful of college classmates, and some of Cheryl's childhood friends.

Kara, Garrett and their two kids drove down from New Jersey. To Ned's surprise, his brother Brian was there with his wife Candice and their twelve year-old daughter Lindsey. He was now a Captain in the Marine Corps and was stationed in San Diego. Prior to the wedding Ned spoke with him for a time. It was the first adult conversation they ever shared. He felt totally at ease with his brother.

Ned's mother, though now showing her age a bit, was nevertheless her spunky self. She reveled in having all of her children together again. She knew that their father would have been proud of each one of them. His memory always added a bittersweet quality to special occasions like this in her children's lives.

"I now pronounce you husband and wife!"

The deed was done in less than a half-hour. They had a simple reception in the basement of the church, changed clothes, and to the cheers of all pulled away from the curb in the Camaro. Their college friends had adorned it with streamers and window graffiti.

Money was tight so they planned only a five-day honeymoon at Rehobeth Beach, on the Delaware coast. It was almost ten in the evening when they pulled into a large motel.

Over the "No Vacancy" sign the marquee was lit up with the words: "Congratulations, Cheryl and Ned."

The honeymoon suite was small but inviting. A living area led to an ornately decorated bedroom. A king-size bed sat in the middle of the room, illuminated by track lighting on the ceiling. Off to the side was a dressing area leading to the bathroom. There, an elevated Jacuzzi tub for two took up most of the room.

Ned could not contain his excitement. "Too bad we won't get to enjoy much of the beach."

Cheryl was tense. She had gotten quiet on the ride to the coast. She spoke for the first time in an hour. "Ned, I'm so tired. Let's just get ready for bed." Without waiting for a reply she grabbed her overnight case and disappeared into the bathroom.

He stepped out of his clothes, turned down the bedcovers, and awaited his bride. Five minutes went by, then ten, and fifteen. The light shone under the door but he heard no noise, no movement. Finally, Ned moved to the door and lightly knocked.

"Cheryl?" No response.

"Are you OK?" No response.

He turned the knob and the door slowly opened. She was sitting atop the commode dressed in a lacy negligee. Her head was in her hands and tears trickled down her cheeks.

He knelt before her and said nothing. She raised her head and looked into his eyes.

"Oh, Ned," she whispered. "You have been saving your-self all your life for this moment. But this is not the first time for me, or the second..."

"I know," he said.

"But, how could you..."

"I can't tell you how, I just knew."

"From the day we met, I haven't wanted to be with another man. I don't deserve…"

He put a finger to her lips. "Ssh."

He took her face in his hands. "My love, neither of us can go back and change the past. But for some reason God has put us together to share a future."

He picked her up in his arms and carried her to the bed. Tenderly they explored one another's bodies. For them there was no longer a past - only the present. They made love until exhaustion overcame them both.

CHAPTER THIRTEEN

Jill was sitting at the kitchen table when Ned returned to the apartment. Coffee was brewing on the counter behind her. He strode in with a burst of energy. Noting his attire she commented, "It looks like you're all dressed up for church."

"As a matter of fact, madam, that's exactly where I've been."

"To church?"

"Yup. It's a good place to clear your head….and your heart."

He deposited a copy of the Sunday New York Times and a white paper bag on the table. "I thought you might like a good old fashioned New York bagel for breakfast. You have a choice of poppy seed, sesame, or rye. And there's cream cheese in the fridge."

Over breakfast he explained that he had spoken with a couple of friends earlier about her husband, and expected to know more by the end of the day.

Shortly after noon they set off for Jill's apartment. It was in a very nice building just north of The Dakota on Central Park West. The doorman opened the cab door for them.

"Good morning, Charles," said Jill.

"Back so soon, Mrs. H?"

Without responding Jill led Ned into the fancy lobby to a first floor rear apartment marked "Manager." The door opened just as she was about to knock. A casually dressed man in his early 50's looked first at Jill and then to Ned.

"Mrs. Hovnanian, is there something I can help you with?"

"Mr. Belamore, someone has stolen my purse and I'll need you to let me in. This friend was kind enough to get me home."

With one more glance at Ned, the super reached in behind the door and grabbed a set of master keys on a large ring. The three of them took an elevator to the seventh floor, and went straight to Apartment #708. The man quickly unlocked the door and left them there.

The apartment was dark. Every drape had been tightly closed. When Jill hit a wall switch she jumped back into Ned's arms. The main room looked like it had been put through a blender. There was nothing undisturbed. The lit lamp lay on the floor projecting eerie shadows across the room.

Ned reached for his pistol holstered in the small of his back. There were no obvious signs of life and they cautiously moved from room to room. The last door led to the master bedroom. He smelled it before they entered – the smell of death. There they found David Hovnanian sprawled on the bed face down. The back of his head had been blown away. Jill's legs gave way and she sank to the floor.

He settled her in a living room chair, and calmly spoke to her.

"I am so sorry, Jill. I don't know how, but I am going to get to the bottom of this. Now, we're going to have to call the police. When they come I want you to tell them everything. All of it, do you understand?"

She nodded. "But what about you?"

"I can take care of myself. To the world I am Richard Carlson. I am a licensed private investigator. Our meeting was providential and now I'm trying to help. I'm sure they will check out all of this with Rivera on San Marcos. Let me explain my own presence there and the name John Henry, which they will no doubt discover. The truth is our greatest ally. Who knows? Maybe New York's "Finest" will figure this out for us. In the meantime, I will do my own investigation. And you can stay at my place. Now, you make the call."

• •

Two patrol officers appeared just minutes after Jill's call. They must have been on foot patrol in Central Park across from the apartment house. The pair looked to Ned like teenagers. *Am I getting that old?* The male, whose nameplate read Kelly, was short and muscular. His partner was a tiny Hispanic female. Her bulky equipment belt seemed to get in the way when she walked.

Despite their age, the officers were very professional. After getting some initial information they secured the crime scene. Sirens could be heard in the distance as motorized units converged on the site. Within twenty minutes the hallway outside the apartment was teeming with uniformed police and criminal technicians.

Kelly and his partner Rodriquez remained with Jill and Ned until two homicide detectives arrived. The lead detective introduced himself as Anthony Valone, and his partner as Marty Brown. Valone was immaculately dressed in a tan suit and striped tie. His shoes had probably been shined that morning. Brown was the fashion opposite of his comrade. His sport coat was wrinkled and his tie stained. It looked like he had slept in his clothes.

Valone was all business. His deep, penetrating eyes seemed to be in a constant searching mode. Ned knew that he and Jill were under intense scrutiny. After concluding that they were going to be cooperative, the detectives arranged for them to be driven to the nearby precinct where they would be interviewed later. It was clear that they wanted to assess the murder scene before it was disturbed any further.

Ned and Jill exchanged no words in the back of the patrol car on their journey to the station house. They were then escorted to separate rooms where they were assigned "baby sitters."

More than two hours elapsed before Valone and Brown reappeared. Ned figured they had already interviewed Jill. They would now be grilling him in hopes of finding inconsistencies in their stories. At least that's how he would have proceeded. They began in a cordial manner.

"Mr. Carlson," said Valone. "We're sorry for the long wait. As you can imagine there are many things to do to get an investigation under way. The trail gets cold very quickly."

Brown joined in. "Can we get you coffee or anything?"

"No," Ned replied. "Officer Perkins has been quite accommodating. Let's get on with this, so that you can do your job."

CHAPTER FOURTEEN

The newlyweds' off-campus apartment was smaller than the honeymoon suite. It was a third floor walkup. All the other tenants were young couples like themselves. On the roof was a barbeque grill for common use, and in the basement a washer and dryer.

Their tuition was paid for the year, but both of them took on part-time jobs to pay for their living expenses. Ned worked at a busy pizzeria in Georgetown three nights a week. Tony from Joe & Pat's back home would have been proud of him. He became a showman as he formed the dough and twirled it high into the air, making a perfect crust every time.

Cheryl did secretarial work in the Psychology Department in the afternoons when she had no classes. They studied hard during the week so that their weekends would be free. They bought her a ten-speed and they spent most Saturdays and many Sunday afternoons exploring Washington and its surrounding areas. Their favorite trip took them up the old C & O Canal bike path which extended for 184 miles, all the way to Cumberland, Maryland. They rarely went beyond Great Falls Park, a distance of about 20 miles.

Life was good.

Both of them were unclear about career choices. In January, a job fair was held at the Student Center. Various companies were represented, as well as several branches of the federal government. The couple wandered through the hall, picking up bits of literature along the way.

About half-way through, they were drawn to a table with a catchy banner overhead. "Join the team! See the world!" At first they thought it might be a recruiting sign for the military, but behind the table sat a young man dressed in a three-piece suit. The table was bare except for a pile of brochures. Cheryl picked one up. Across the top it read "The United States of America Department of State. The man noted her surprise.

"I'd be glad to answer any questions."

They turned to him. Ned playfully asked, "And what might you be selling today?"

"I haven't been asked that much this morning," the man responded. "I think it's the banner. People think I'm a Navy recruiter masquerading in civilian clothes. My name is Ben Kazinski, and I do work for the State Department, the Diplomatic Corps to be more precise. Will you let me practice my sales pitch on you?"

For the next forty-five minutes they sat across the table from Ben, listening intently to his words. When he finished, he asked them, "How did I do?"

"I'd give you an A," said Cheryl. "Do you ever hire married couples?"

"No," he said *diplomatically*. "But if you each qualify, you may both be hired. We have many couples serving together overseas. They are some of our most stable assignments. It's not easy to get in, but for the right people, it's a great life."

With that Ben reached under the table and retrieved two manila folders filled with papers. His business card was stapled to each one.

"In here my friends, is all you need to know about us, and forms to tell us all we need to know about you. If you are really interested, call me personally when you've completed them. I sense this could be a start of an adventure for the two of you."

Ned and Cheryl immediately left the hall. They had some reading to do.

• •

Within a few weeks they submitted their applications. They took some preparatory tests and had interviews with several individuals. Ben Kaminski was true to his word, guiding and encouraging them through the entire process.

By graduation in May they had offers in hand to begin work on July 1st. They quit their part-time jobs, scraped together all their savings, and took the Camaro on its final trip. They followed their love for the mountains to the Berkshires in Massachusetts, the White Mountains of New Hampshire, and the Green of Vermont. The last week they stayed on the coast of Maine.

They slept each night in an 8 X 10 pop-up tent which they nicknamed "Tara." An air-mattress and a double sleeping bag kept them warm and dry, though they awoke to temperatures in the 30's several mornings. After briefly visiting family on the way back, they attended a church retreat near Camp David and arrived home just two days before the start of work.

Refreshed and deeply tanned, they reported for duty on Wednesday, July 1, 1985. With sixteen others they were ushered into a conference room. The Secretary of State himself awaited them. After a few comments he took his leave, and to their surprise the new trainees were asked to give both an oral and written pledge of allegiance to the country. It was a sobering moment.

The training leader distributed a syllabus that outlined no less than six months of orientation and specialized learning.

"So much for the end of school," Ned murmured to his wife.

They began with a tour of the facility, fire safety, a review of policies and procedures, an explanation of benefits, and a litany of U.S. laws governing their employment. All together they would spend one year at headquarters before being assigned as deputies in some foreign embassy.

After answering some questions, their leader made note of the fact after just three days of work they would get their first holiday off. With a sly smile he said, "Not bad for government work."

By October their training courses were scheduled less frequently, and Ned and Cheryl were assigned to separate offices within the massive complex. Every day they would meet for lunch, often joining hundreds of others outside to enjoy the early fall in the nation's capitol. It seemed that every day they had more to share as each of them was being given more responsibility in their work.

One weekend Cheryl stayed in bed most of the time. For a couple of weeks she felt like she was fighting off some kind of a bug. On Monday morning she could hardly drag herself in to work, and vomited in the Ladies Room shortly after arriving. One of her coworkers, a jolly grandmotherly type named Beatrice, was washing up at the sink when Cheryl came out of the stall.

"You all right, child?"

"I'll be OK," she responded. "It's just a bug or something."

"I've been watching you for a while girl. My guess is you've got more than some bug inside you. My radar is pretty accurate in these things. I'll bet you're pregnant."

"Yeah, right. Thanks for the insight there, Bea."

As the day progressed Cheryl felt much better, but she hadn't forgotten Beatrice's words. *What would we do if it were true?*

That evening she went down to the apartment below to see Donna, who had become a good friend over the past year. She told her about her experience, and about Bea's comment.

"Well, lady. There's only one way to find out, isn't there? Nurse Donna has just the thing for you." She disappeared for a moment and returned with a small box with pink and blue lettering.

"This is a spare that I've been saving. Take it and use it." She handed her the home pregnancy kit. Cheryl's hands shook as she held it in her hands.

The next morning Cheryl looked in amazement at the little strip she held in her hands. Ned came into the bathroom to get something. He stared at her, staring at it. And then they stared at one another. He was speechless, she was not.

"Ned, I think we've created a new life."

CHAPTER FIFTEEN

The two detectives took chairs opposite Ned at a table. Brown opened a notebook and assumed the position of recording secretary. At the same time Valone placed a small recording device in front of him.

"I hope you don't mind if we record our session here," Mr. Carlson. "It's for your protection as well as ours."

"Please call me Rich. And no, I don't mind the recording."

After dictating the date, time and the principals in the room, Valone asked Ned to relate everything that happened, from the incident in the cantina to the discovery of David Hovnanian's body. Ned obliged by giving a very detailed account of the previous two days. The detective's gaze was constant, his mind fully engaged. When Ned finished, the questioning took a different tack. He had anticipated this.

"Your observation skills are excellent, Rich. We may have to ask you to run through it again later. But there are a few more things that we have to ask. They will help us fill in some blanks."

Brown took over. Ned had almost forgotten that he was in the room.

"Mr....Rich, could you tell us how long you've been a P.I.?"

"I assumed you guys would have checked me out already. I've been in business for a little more than twenty years. I work out of my home. My clients are almost all corporate."

"Business has been good?"

"Very good, detective. I have made a good living."

The three of them were momentarily distracted as a moth flew out of the lighting fixture and moved uncertainly around the room before it settled on a large mirrored window. Marty Brown brought things back into focus: "Rich, are you licensed to carry a firearm?"

"You must know that. I surrendered my gun to the officers at the apartment."

Brown hestitated. "Yes, of course. Now sir, would you mind telling us what you were doing on San Marcos? It appears you had been there for some time."

"Seven months, gentlemen. How much vacation time do you get each year?"

"I don't see how this relates to my question…"

"I assume you probably get five or six weeks. Well, I haven't had a real vacation since I started in business. I thought that I had a nice, long one coming. I could afford it, and San Marcos was the perfect spot. You would love it."

"I'm sure I would."

Brown seemed uneasy, like the flow of the interview had been taken from him. Valone too noticed this and stepped in.

"Rich, is there anything else we should know about your *vacation*?

"No, it was very relaxing and uneventful, until the other night. I'm sure you will be checking with Chief Rivera down there. By the way, he's retired N.Y.P.D. I don't think he'll have much to add, though I'm sure he isn't happy about our hasty departure. But under the circumstances we felt we had to get away from there."

"Anything else?"

"One thing. The Chief knew me as John Henry. It was part of my break from my work. I didn't want any of my clients trying to track me down for any more work."

Valone thought he might have something here. His eyes focused squarely on Ned.

"Rich, people usually don't change their names unless they have something to hide. What are you not telling us?"

"Nothing sinister. I just wanted to be left alone for some R & R. My life is an open book. *They should only know.*

"You never met Jill Hovnanian until the other night?"

"No."

"And you just took up her cause?"

"I saw it more as saving her life."

"And why do you continue to help her, Rich? She's even staying at your apartment here in New York."

Valone was good, and he was beginning to annoy Ned.

He responded, "Listen! This moved from 'damsel in distress' to something much more personal when her pursuers tried to use my home as a barbeque grill. So yes, I am going to continue to help her until this thing is solved. And frankly, detectives, I hope that you will figure it out. You've got all the resources."

"OK, Rich, that's fair enough, for now. But I caution you that this is our murder investigation. If we find you interfering in any way, we will come down hard on you. And don't plan on doing any more vacationing for a while."

With that, Brown closed his notebook, Valone picked up the recorder, and the two of them left the room.

· ·

It was early evening when Jill and Ned left the precinct. There was a light rain falling, though the temperature was still quite mild. They began walking south toward Columbus

Circle. Everyone had taken their business indoors, so they seemed all alone.

They understood one another's need for some silence. Her nerves were at the breaking point. Her husband was dead, and she didn't know how to react. She had not as yet shed any tears. She was sure that this was duly noted by the detectives.

What do I feel? Sadness? Grief? Relief?

Ned was lost in his own thoughts. Life was suddenly turned on end. It seemed like a month since he left San Marcos. Would he go back some day? But there was also a raw excitement about being back in New York, and back in the game. Was this something new, or a return to the old? And what about this attractive woman walking beside him? He would not take advantage of her vulnerability, but with her he was beginning to feel a bit vulnerable himself.

They found an open coffee shop near Fordham University and sat in a booth by the window. Though they hadn't eaten in many hours, neither of them was hungry. They ordered coffee and pie.

He broke the ice. "How was it for you back there, Jill"

"I told them everything, just like you said to. I don't know if they believed me or not. They asked a lot about our marriage. I was as honest as I could be."

"Good, they can usually tell when someone is holding back."

"What now, Ned?"

"First, you owe me a dollar."

"Why?"

"That's my retainer to be your own private investigator. If I don't spend it all, I'll refund what's left."

That brought a smile to her face. "So this is how you amassed your wealth."

"Yes, one dollar at a time."

"What else?"

"You have a funeral to arrange, and I have to keep you safe until someone is put in jail. And, I am going to work your case like a pit bull."

"I can't go back to that apartment."

"They wouldn't let you, anyway. Besides, your trigger-happy friends would know right where to find you. Plan to stay at my place for now."

They took an Eighth Avenue Local down to Union Station and walked to his apartment from there. The walking drained some of the tension from the day. After setting the locks on the door, Ned turned around to find Jill close to him.

She tipped her head and asked, "Is it against the rules for a client to give her P.I. a hug?"

"I'll have to look it up."

They held each other for a long time.

CHAPTER SIXTEEN

Once they got over the shock, Cheryl and Ned Reed were excited over the prospect of being parents. Other than those first weeks, Cheryl enjoyed a trouble-free pregnancy. Between work and other pursuits they remained very busy. Slowly they transformed their spare room from home office to nursery. They painted the walls yellow in anticipation of a boy or a girl. They spent hours musing over names, changing their minds on choices many times.

By late Spring the couple had completed their childhood and parenting classes. Cheryl's OB-GYN started seeing her every week in anticipation of a delivery within the month.

Three weeks before her due-date, Cheryl made the hour's drive to her parent's home one Saturday morning. She and her mother planned a shopping spree for last minute baby things. By six that evening, Ned began to worry. He called his in-laws who told him that she had left at four in the afternoon. He tried her pager again. By seven he couldn't wait any longer. He arranged to borrow a neighbor's car so that he could retrace the route to the Blaine's.

He got no further than the front steps. There he was met by two uniformed officers. One of them asked. "Could you tell us which one is the Reed apartment?"

"I'm Ned Reed," he said.

"Mr. Reed, your wife has been in an accident."

He felt weak. "Is she all right?"

"We don't know. We've been instructed to bring you over to Sibley Hospital as quickly as possible."

· ·

The patrol car pulled up to the Emergency Room entrance and Ned was out of the car before it came to a stop. He ran to the admission desk and the woman behind the counter calmly asked the name of the patient. He was beside himself. She made a call and when she hung up she told him that a doctor would be right out to speak with him. The doors to the treatment area opened immediately and a young man in a white smock strode up to Ned.

"Please follow me, Mr. Reed."

"But..."

"We don't have time to talk now. Please come!"

Ned followed him down the hallway into a waiting elevator. There on a gurney lay his wife, bloodied and battered. Bottles and tubes hung everywhere. She was barely conscious and moaning in pain. Ned grabbed her hand and made eye contact with her. She mouthed the words, "I love you."

The doors opened and he kissed Cheryl as she was being torn away from him. The young doctor took Ned by the elbow and ushered him into a small conference room.

"Mr. Reed..."

"What happened?" Ned demanded.

"I don't know all the details. What I do know is that your wife was involved in a very serious auto accident. The other driver did not survive. Mrs. Reed is severely injured and is bleeding internally. The surgeons are going to do their best."

Ned shook his head as if trying to wake from a dream. "Our baby?"

"Let's let them do their work, sir. They will tell us as soon as they can. Is there anyone we can call?"

• •

Hours went by. Cheryl's parents joined Ned in the surgical waiting room. Their neighbors Donna and Phil also came. Someone also called the church because Tom Wade was there before anyone else. A social worker brought coffee. There was little conversation in the room.

Finally the door opened and a weary surgeon, hat in hand, stood before them. "Mr. Reed," he said, "I am so sorry. We did everything we could, but it wasn't enough."

Ned collapsed in a chair.

"Sir, we could not save your wife, but we were able to save your daughter."

"My daughter?"

"She appears to be a healthy baby girl. We'll know more after she's been thoroughly examined."

"Grace," Ned said.

"I don't understand," the physician replied.

"Her name is Grace, doctor. Our daughter's name is Grace."

• •

Ned Reed would remember only one thing from the day his wife died. It was the instant that he saw his daughter's face for the first time. The nurses in the neo-natal unit outfitted him in cap, gown and gloves. Then they sat him in a rocking chair, brought Grace to him wrapped in a pink blanket, and left them alone.

In those moments Ned whispered words to his daughter that only she would ever hear. It was with great reluctance

that the head nurse finally interrupted them in order to attend
to the baby's needs.

CHAPTER SEVENTEEN

N ed was just dozing off around midnight when his cell phone rang. It was one of his contacts. "Rich, it's Kevin. I know it's late but you said to call as soon as I had something for you."

"It's OK. What do you have?"

"First, you didn't say I'd be checking on a corpse."

"Kevin, I didn't know he was dead until this afternoon."

"I figured you'd still want to know about this guy. I pulled a few strings and some things unraveled. Your Mr. Hovnanian has, or should I say, had an office just off of Lexington Avenue. His company goes by the name Old World Trading Company. It's some kind of wholesale import-export house, mostly imports. He is listed as the owner/proprietor, but when I looked deeper I came across a trail of related companies. The more you dig the muddier it gets. I suspect your man was fronting for some heavy hitters. I've seen this kind of thing before."

"Any idea what they were dealing in?"

"No, Rich. And I suspect it won't be easy to find out. On the surface, he was supposed to be importing exotic furnishings and carpets. I bet you won't find any warehouses anywhere."

"Is that it?"

"One more thing. This guy was on the road a lot. In the last six months or so he made numerous trips abroad, mostly to North Africa and the Middle East."

"Where did you get that information?"

"Trade secrets, *amigo*. I have my sources. Anyway, that's all I can give you right now. If I get any more I'll let you know."

"Thanks Kevin. You'll find your reward in the usual place."

• •

Ned was now wide-awake. He sat reading and rereading his notes from the phone conversation. In the margin he had written the address Kevin had given him. By morning he was certain the police would be all over David's office. He knew that he couldn't wait.

He was dressed and out the door in ten minutes, taking a knapsack with him. The skies had cleared, and he marveled that there were still people out in the wee hours of the morning. He walked along a bus route until an Uptown bus appeared. Shortly he was standing before a narrow three-story building, separated by taller ones on either side by narrow alleys. On the street level it housed a travel agency. A metal grating was pulled across the front and locked with a formidable combination lock.

There was just enough illumination from the streetlights for him to see the words "Old World" on a third-floor front window. He gazed around. The street was deserted. He moved down the alley closest to the window. Removing a flashlight from his bag he peered up the side of the building. Suspended high above him was a retractable fire-escape set in the up position.

He pulled out a reel-type device and opened a claw at its end. With a flick of his wrist he sent the claw skyward. It hit the ironwork but did not find a solid hold. The metallic noise pierced the night. He waited a moment. Again, he cast the claw and this time it gripped a horizontal piece. He pulled it quickly to stop any vibration.

Putting on a pair of thin leather gloves, he gripped the line and lifted his body hand over hand until he could extend a leg over the rail of the fire-escape. Perched there, he found himself opposite a third-story window. Taking the flashlight again he surveyed the window for alarms. Finding none, he prepared to use a glass cutter to gain access, when he realized that the lock was in the open position.

It was less than five minutes from when he entered the alley, and he was already standing in what appeared to be a vacant office. It took him a moment to realize that the room he was seeking was next door. Unlocking the door, he entered a dimly lit hallway. David Hovnanian's office door was ajar. Pushing it open with one hand, he shined the flashlight into the darkness with the other.

Furniture and files were strewn everywhere. Closing the window blinds he switched on the ceiling light, and began moving through the room, looking for anything the previous visitors overlooked. Just as he was about to give up, his eyes were drawn to a ceiling tile above the door which was slightly askew. Standing on a chair he raised the tile and felt around in all directions. His fingers finally touched something wrapped in plastic.

He sat in a chair and stared at what appeared to be a small ledger book. Stuffing it into his sack, he retraced his steps through the other office. He climbed out the window, re-closed it, and slid down the line to the alley below. Whipping the line into the air he released the claw and replaced everything in his backpack.

Slipping back into his apartment, Ned checked on Jill. She was breathing heavily in sleep. Depositing his clothes on a chair in his bedroom he placed the bag under his bed, slipped between the covers, and extinguished the light. The alarm clock read 1:42 am.

CHAPTER EIGHTEEN

The last time Ned had entered a funeral home was when he was ten years old. In the midst of hundreds of family members and well-wishers he felt like that frightened little boy again. There were conversations going on all around him, but his thoughts were far away. He refocused again when a man, someone he didn't recognize, grasped his hand.

"Mr. Reed, I'm John Reister. Cheryl and I were friends in high school. I'm sorry for your loss. She was such a special person."

"Thank you for coming, John. Yes, she was."

The man squeezed his hand again. "I guess the Lord wanted her more than we did."

Ned's reaction was immediate. He pushed the man back into a wall and went face to face with him. Everyone in the room was drawn to the commotion and suddenly there was complete silence.

"How dare you presume to know the will of God! Do you think it was God's will that the other driver drank a dozen beers that day? Do you think it was God's will that he got behind the wheel of a car? Do you think it was the will of God that Cheryl was in that intersection the moment he ran the red light? Do you?"

He left the questions hanging, released the man, and left the room.

· ·

Bill Campbell conducted a powerful but sensitive funeral service. The God he spoke about shared Ned's sadness and grief, and it was a great comfort to him. Individuals were given the opportunity to share memories of Cheryl. There were many tears as well as many smiles. Ned insisted that Grace be present. He sat with her nestled in his arms, and she slept the entire time.

After the burial service Ned arranged to meet alone with his sister Kara and her husband Garrett. They sat in the coffee shop which was attached to the motel where they were staying. The three of them were emotionally drained from the events of the previous three days. They sat quietly for a time sipping their coffee.

Ned had an agenda. "Kara, Garrett. I haven't slept in 72 hours. I have been thinking about Cheryl and worrying about Grace. I have something to ask of you. I'll understand if your answer is *no*. So let me come right out with it. Would you consider raising our baby as your own?"

There was silence.

"Do you know what you're proposing, little brother?" his sister asked.

"I have no right to ask this of you…"

"No, you misunderstand. It's not about us. It's about you, and Grace."

"She deserves much more than I can give her. I'm a broken man, Kara. I have nothing to offer her but a life of uncertainty. And you guys have the most loving family I've ever seen."

Garrett had said nothing to this point. Now he leaned toward his brother-in-law.

"Ned, we are not afraid of raising another child. We've even talked about having another of our own. But if we do this, it's got to be forever…..legal adoption, the whole thing. There can never be an emotional tug of war at Grace's expense."

The two held eye contact. "I understand. I will never stop loving her, but I promise that I will not interfere."

And so the die was cast. Grace Ann Reed, became Grace Ann Dickson, the youngest child of Kara and Garrett, and sister to Adam, Brett, and Allison.

Ned Francis Reed was adrift in the world again.

• •

He was back to work the following week. He rarely left his apartment once he returned home from the office each day. Every night he would fall asleep exhausted, only to awake at three or four in the morning.

About six months after the accident that took Cheryl's life, Ned got a call one afternoon from Ben Kazinski, the man who had brought the two of them into the State Department.

"Ned, we haven't talked in a while. How are you?"

"I'm surviving Ben. I can't say much more than that."

"Are you doing anything special for supper tonight?"

"No. I haven't selected my TV dinner yet."

"Will you join me? My treat? I have something I want to run by you."

"I'm not very good company these days, Ben."

"Just say yes, as a favor to a friend."

"OK."

Ben came by Ned's office at about five. They took a short cab ride to the Metropolitan Café where Ben had reserved a table. It hadn't been necessary, for there were only a few other patrons at that early hour. After some awkward small talk, Ben got down to business.

"Ned, as you know, I've taken a personal interest in you and Cheryl from the start. You were my star recruits. I can't imagine the hell you've been going through."

"Thanks, Ben. Life has to go on I guess."

"That's why I invited you out tonight. As you know, you are due for your final performance evaluation next month."

"I haven't given it any thought."

"I'm not surprised. The fact is, Ned, that though you have been doing your work, everyone has noticed a difference in you. You no longer take any initiative. I read one comment which used the phrase "going through the motions.""

"I didn't think it was *that* obvious."

"The bottom line is that I don't think you will be very happy with the bosses' plans for you. It may be time to consider other options."

"Do I have any other options, Ben?"

"There is someone I want you to meet. It involves another job within the government, but you would be with an agency that works, shall we say, below the radar."

"It sounds mysterious. But I'm not sure I can handle any more change in my life right now, Ben."

"Change is coming, my friend. That's why I'm giving you a heads up, so that you can have some control over what happens."

"I don't know…."

"You have nothing to lose. Just talk to this guy. After that, you decide. Let me make the call for you?"

Ned felt a surge of energy he had not experienced in some time. "OK. I'll listen to what he has to say."

That night Ned had a dream. He was riding on the Carousel at South Beach Amusement Park. Round and round he went, watching others as they lunged for the gold ring mounted just out of reach. Then he was no longer a spectator. With one hand on the pole and only one foot on a stirrup, he threw himself aloft and plucked a shiny brass ring out of the air.

When he awoke it was 7:30 in the morning. He had slept through the night for the first time in six months.

CHAPTER NINETEEN

Every Monday morning a sleepy city emerges from its brief respite to rekindle the flames of commerce and industry. Before dawn, the highways, bridges, and tunnels begin to fill with vehicles from the outer boroughs and New Jersey. Trains from Long Island, Connecticut and the Northern suburbs swell with commuters. Ferries, buses, and subways all converge on a narrow island named for the Manhattan Indians who once hunted wild game, where concrete and steel now dominated the landscape. Coffee shops and street corner vendors display their offerings of flavored coffees, rolls, bagels and Danish. The noise builds to a crescendo during the aptly named rush hour.

There are pockets of calm in neighborhoods tucked away from commercial districts and thoroughfares. Few people owned cars in Ned's area of The Village. Many of the residents lived alternative life-styles that had them working nights and sleeping days.

Across from his brownstone was a small park. Ned and Jill sat opposite one another at a concrete table used by chess players each afternoon. The remains of their breakfast lay in wrappers set off to the side. They were examining his find from the night before.

"I can't believe you actually went there last night. You took a big risk. I thought the police told you to let them handle the investigation."

"I'm not going to sit by while people are still looking for us, Jill."

"It's *us* now? You can still walk away from this."

"That's not an option for me anymore, for many reasons."

She looked at him intently. "I trust you," she said. "But I'm not sure why. All I know is that you are very handsome, and that your name is Ned, or John, or Richard. You seem to be independently wealthy. You are considerate, and you go to church. You are also fearless and inventive. You give good hugs. And for some reason you were there to save my life…..twice. *And,* you seem to be willing to help me wherever that leads."

"Say more about that handsome part."

"I'm not joking, Ned. I want to know who you are. Really!"

"Maybe we can have that conversation some day, Jill. But not right now. It's enough that you trust me. Let's get through this, and if you're still so curious about me later, we'll see about the rest. Right this moment I need you to look at this book." He handed her his treasure from the night before.

She thumbed through the pages slowly, more than fifty of them, filled with names and numbers.

"Do you recognize anything, Jill?"

"Nothing," she said, shaking her head.

"Not even one name? Could you have taken a phone message from someone here?"

"I'm sorry. I can't remember a single business call coming to our home. I told you, David was very secretive about his work."

"Unless I'm mistaken, the key to his murder and your troubles is right here in front of us."

"Shouldn't you turn it over to the police?"

He closed the book. "Not yet. Not until I understand what it means."

• •

From the park Ned led her to an office supply store where he carefully photocopied each page of the ledger. Next he stopped by a nearby branch of Chase Bank and placed the original in a safety-deposit box which was rented under the name of Carlton Avery. When Jill heard him give that name to the bank representative, it took total self-control to contain her laughter. *Another name for my collection.*

On the way home she playfully took Ned's arm. "O Carlton," she said. "You are such a tease. When will you tell me the truth? Your real name is James Bond, isn't it? Or perhaps, Clark Kent, or Bruce Wayne?"

She let her arm remain there and he did not object. His months of solitude now seemed far in the past. He was beginning to feel alive again. Maybe he was on the road back. The misdeeds of his professional life, often guided by twisted loyalty and logic, no longer consumed his thoughts. Maybe there was a future.

Outside the brownstone, Ned turned to Jill and kissed her lightly on the lips. "Thank you," he said softly.

"For what?"

He didn't answer.

Soon he had copies of the ledger book spread out across the kitchen counter. He had scanned the entries briefly the night before, but now began to study them in earnest. One column was evidently a list of dates starting about three years before. They were written in a European format with the day, month and year noted, rather than with the month first. For instance, the first entry was made on 18.7.05.

In the second column were a series of names, dozens of them. Ned assumed that these were all business contacts of David Hovnanian. Many of the names were repeated several times. Remembering Kevin's report that David had been traveling extensively in Eastern Europe and the Middle East, he was not surprised to see surnames like Andropov, Sherakova, Aziz and Hadad. On later pages he noted more use of first names like Sergei, Tarik, Ludmilla and Ahmed.

The meaning of the long numbers in the final column, were less clear to Ned. Some of them had decimal points which could have indicated monetary amounts. Others had dashes which could have connoted account or part numbers, or perhaps even phone numbers. Next to several of the Slavic names, the first three numbers were 718. Ned was sure that this was the area code for Brooklyn, where a large population of Russians had settled in Brighton Beach. It was also the home turf of the Russian mafia in the United States. He felt that he now had a place to start.

Jill entered the room dressed in a terry-cloth robe, busily drying her hair with a towel. For a moment he was mesmerized. Her motions and mannerisms transported him to another time more than twenty years earlier. He hadn't thought of Cheryl in a long time.

Jill brought him back quickly to the present. "Find out anything, big boy?"

"As a matter of fact I have. I have a lot of things to do now. I know it will be hard for you to stay right here, but I don't want you outside any more than necessary. You have the TV, a bookcase full of good reading material, and anything you might want to concoct in the kitchen."

"How long will I have to be cooped up here?"

"I don't know Jill. But you'll have to promise me you'll let me handle this my way."

"Aye, aye, sir," she offered, making a stiff salute.

CHAPTER TWENTY

Two days after his dinner with Ben, Ned decided to take a brisk walk during the lunch hour. The air was cool and dry. Heading in the direction of the Capitol Building, he was almost immediately joined by a stranger in a conservative suit and tie.

"Mr. Reed, do you mind if I join you?"

At the sound of his name, Ned stopped and looked at the man. "Do I know you?"

"No, but we have a mutual friend – Ben Kazinski."

"So you are the one I was to hear from?"

"That's right. Sam Parker is my name." They resumed their walk.

"Mr. Parker, I don't know what Ben has told you about me, but I'm not sure if I'm up to any career moves right now."

"Ned, I know everything about you from the day you entered the world up to the current time."

"That sounds a bit weird. How would you have gotten all that information? And the real question is 'Why'?

"The *how* is not so difficult. The *why* may be a little harder to explain. Let's just say our agency is very selective in our choice of potential employees, and you meet the criteria quite well."

"And they would be…?"

"Intelligent, independent, healthy, principled, patriotic, and unattached."

"That doesn't sound like me."

"Oh yes. I forgot to mention unassuming."

"I'm listening, Mr. Parker."

"It's Sam."

They found a park bench and sat facing one another. For the next thirty minutes Sam Parker laid out a possible career scenario for him. Ned didn't interrupt him even once.

When he finished, Sam asked if Ned had any questions.

"You haven't told me the name of this agency."

"I can't do that yet. Not until you are on board and in training."

"Who is it accountable to?"

"I can say without hesitation that our work is authorized at the very highest level of our government."

Ned smiled. "I'm not sure if you just answered that question or not. Who would decide what my assignments would be?"

"You ask insightful questions. I can't answer that one because I don't know myself. I do know that these decisions are made based on national security concerns, and by representatives within the Executive and Legislative branches of our government. It's not important for us to know specifically who those persons are."

"What if I'm told to do something ethical or illegal?"

"First let me say Ned, that you have been chosen *because* you are both an ethical and a just person. In this very dangerous world, however, it is necessary to recognize that not everything is black and white. Sometimes things have to be done to avert tragedy or harm to our nation and its citizens. At those times we rely on people with integrity who can put everything into perspective and do what has to be done."

Glancing at his watch Ned realized that it was already well beyond his lunch hour. "Mr. Parker, I have to go. But I will think about your proposal. How can I contact you?"

"I will contact you, Ned, within forty-eight hours."

"That's not a lot of time to consider such heady things."

"Experience tells us that you will know in less time than that whether you will invest your life in what I'm proposing."

They shook hands.

By the time Ned reached his desk, he had made a decision.

****

Just three days after Ned's walk in the park with Sam Parker, his office at the State Department was empty. No one seemed to know where he went. His work-load was reassigned to another person. In a matter of weeks, he would be just a memory to those who had worked closely with him.

The apartment that Ned had occupied for two years also was vacated. In the middle of the night all of his belongings disappeared. The landlord was paid in cash for what remained of the lease. Confused neighbors speculated on Ned's fate. Most of them finally concluded that, never really getting over Cheryl's death, he probably decided to make a clean break with the past and begin life anew in some other place.

Ned's only phone call was to Kara. After inquiring about Gracie's well-being, he told his sister that he had the opportunity to take on a new government assignment, and that it would involve constant travel. He assured her that he was OK and that he would be in touch from time to time.

His new home was a cottage on the grounds of the F.B.I. Training Center in Quantico, Virginia. He had only two house-mates. One was another trainee he knew only as

Alpha. He was a short, stocky fellow who could be mistaken for a construction worker or a plumber. He had dark features, and his hands and feet were large in proportion to the rest of his body. Ned's name for training purposes was Beta. The two were instructed to share their backgrounds with one another only in general terms.

The other member of the household was a man named Isaiah Robinson. He was their training instructor. An African-American in his early forties, he was the epitome of a Marine Drill Instructor. With shoulders twice the width of his waist, short-cropped hair, immaculate grooming, and a resonant deep voice, he was a presence with which to be reckoned.

Ned discovered that it was not only F.B.I. recruits that came to Quantico for training. Law Enforcement personnel from around the country took courses in specialty areas from the instructors there. Classroom work for him and Alpha, however, was limited. They participated with other trainees in physical conditioning and weapon training. But they had their own private tutor in Isaiah Robinson. What they learned from him wasn't taught in any classroom at the academy. When he was finished with them they would be mentally and emotionally prepared to blend into any world culture. They would speak Russian, Arabic, and Spanish flawlessly.

Finally Ned knew the government agency for whom he was working. Its funding couldn't be found in any budget. Its employees, totaling less than a hundred, were listed on no government payrolls. They simply did not exist. They were the highly trained operatives of T.R.U.T.H., the Tactical Response Unit for The Homeland.

CHAPTER TWENTY-ONE

By mid-afternoon Ned had the address of a Russian social club in Coney Island to which the majority of the calls were made by David Hovnanian. He waited until early evening and took a cab to the predominantly Russian immigrant neighborhood. Stores and offices were covered with signs that few Americans could read. The sidewalks were filled with people of all ages. The smell of unusual blends of tobacco hung in the air as Ned passed small groups of men gathered outside storefronts or on street corners. If he didn't know better he would have thought that he was in a middle-class neighborhood in Moscow or Kiev.

The social club was in the middle of a block. The windows were covered on the inside by thick drapes. The steel door was full of Russian graffiti, and there were no signs to indicate what might lie beyond it. Ned rapped boldly on the door. After a short interval it opened, and a heavy-set man with a bushy mustache, peeked his head outside. "Da" was all he said.

In perfect Russian Ned asked to see Mr. Andropov. The door closed again and he waited several moments before it reopened. The same man led him through a large hall filled with tables of men. Bottles of Vodka were evident everywhere. As he moved through an eerie silence enveloped the room. They climbed a rear stairway and paused before a closed door. The man had Ned face the wall and he was patted down for weapons.

He was shown into a large office where three men were sitting, one of them behind an enormous wooden desk which had seen better days. This man eyed Ned for a moment and then asked him in Russian, "To what do we owe the pleasure of your company? It's Mr. Henry, isn't it? I understand that your Russian is excellent, but why don't we stick to English?"

"Am I speaking to Mr. Andropov?"

"At your service. You realize that you have made a foolish mistake by coming here. It's possible that you could just.....disappear."

Ned looked at him fearlessly. "Since you know who I am, you also know that I would not be here if I didn't know something about you, some information that affords me a measure of safety for the moment. I believe I am in possession of something you want. It is something that you couldn't find at an apartment on the West Side of Manhattan or an office in Midtown."

"You are very good, Mr. Henry. Mrs. Hovnanian was fortunate to have found you. Now what is it that you want?"

"It's very simple. I want you to leave her alone. She had no knowledge of her husband's business. She wants to just go on with her life."

"How can I know this is so? Especially now, since she is apparently in possession of property that is mine."

"Correction, Andropov. I am in possession of this property, not her. She has no idea what this is about, and she doesn't know I am here. All she knows is that her husband is dead, and someone is trying to kill her also."

"Assuming all this is true, it could be easily resolved if you just give me what I am looking for."

"It is true, but I came today to tell you that your secrets are safe as long as no harm comes to her or to me. I don't know what her husband was doing for you, but he obviously betrayed you in some way. It can all end with his death."

"Give me what is mine, Mr. Henry!"

"And sign our death warrants? I don't think so. Consider this: if anything happens to either of us, your property, as you call it, will be handed over to the proper authorities."

The Russian's face was turning red. "You underestimate me."

"On the contrary, I believe you are very powerful and dangerous. That's why I offer this solution which will protect both of us."

"I will consider your proposal. But be very careful, Mr. Henry. You are on very shaky ground here."

"So are you, Mr. Andropov. But this can work if you will agree to it."

"Come here tomorrow evening then, about the same time."

"No, I will call you by phone, and you can give me your answer."

Ned turned and left the room, marching out of the club with his escort in tow. When the outside door slammed behind him, he let out a gasp of air. He was certain that he had just dodged a bullet.

• •

Jill opened the door when she heard the key in the latch. Ned had been gone for several hours. To his surprise, standing behind her in the living room was Detective Valone, as well as another male and a female.

She was obviously flustered. "I couldn't tell them when you'd be back, so they decided to wait."

"What a wonderful surprise, Detective. If I knew you were coming I would have stopped and picked up some donuts."

"Very funny, Mr. Carlson. It seems we have reached an impasse in our investigation, and you appear to be the reason."

"I can't imagine why, Detective."

"Then I'll explain. First let me introduce Special Agents McKenna and Fowler from the F.B.I.. They appeared on our doorstep as soon as David Hovnanian's death became public. It seems that he has been a person of interest of theirs for some time."

"OK. But what has this got to do with me?"

"Since yesterday we have been checking on you. We have discovered that you really don't exist. Not even our colleagues here have been able to identify you. Then earlier this afternoon we were contacted by the National Security Agency to tell us to stop our enquiries regarding you, and that we should enlist you as a resource in our probe. You are apparently a VIP, Mr. Carlson, if that is who you are."

"I'm flattered. I'll help any way I can."

Valone continued. "I'm not sure just how valuable you will be to our murder investigation, but it seems the feds have other things to discuss with you. So I'll leave them with you for now. I can contact you later if I need you."

As soon as the Detective left, the F.B.I. Agents, who had not uttered a word to this point, assumed their roles. Ned sensed that they had been holding back until they had him and Jill alone. The female, Fowler, took the lead.

"Mr. Carlson, the Bureau is not accustomed to working with unidentified strangers. Our presence here should tell you that what we are investigating is extremely important. Our instructions from on high do not ease our discomfort, but for some reason you are someone with whom we will have to cooperate."

It was Ned's turn to voice reservations. "Agents, all I can tell you is that we are on the same side. My involvement in this case is entirely coincidental, but since I am involved, I will see it through."

McKenna joined the conversation. Turning toward Jill, he said, "There is also the matter of Mrs. Hovnanian. Pardon our talking about you as if you weren't here, but you also present a problem for us. Mr. Carlson…"

"You might as well call me Rich if we are going to be partners."

"OK, Rich. In that case I am Mike, and this is Kate. Now about Mrs. Hovnanian. She represents a possible witness for us, but she may also be a suspect. We are not sure she should be privy to what we have to discuss with you."

Again Ned had to explain Jill's plight, this time to the good guys. "I have been with this woman almost constantly for the last three days. I have observed and questioned her extensively, and as you yourselves will see, her only mistake was to marry the wrong man. Her value as a witness will be limited, but you will have to determine that. As far as being a suspect, I ruled that out long ago, as you will also. Now like it or not, we need her to be involved in this. Her life depends on it. You'll have to take my word for that."

Fowler looked to her partner and then to Ned. "Rich, before we do anything, I have to clear this with our superiors. Bringing a civilian into an investigation like this is highly irregular, and perhaps risky. Excuse me…"

She produced a cell phone and disappeared into the rear bedroom. The three others engaged in small talk until she emerged ten minutes later.

"I am not sure of this," she said, "but it seems your opinion carries a good bit of weight, Mr. Carlson. She is on board. But if at any time we deem her involvement detrimental, we reserve the right to change the rules."

"Fair enough," Ned responded. "Now since we are on a first name basis, how about calling her Jill."

CHAPTER TWENTY-TWO

N ed spent more than a year at Quantico. For 12 to 14 hours a day he was honed, physically and mentally, into an instrument of T.R.U.T.H. When F.B.I. recruits were tucked away in their barracks for the night, in the cottage Isaiah Robinson taught Alpha and Beta about international politics or living with multiple identities. The only times they left the base were on "field trips" to D.C., Richmond, and Baltimore, where they practiced their new found skills in real life situations.

Near the end of their training they also made brief trips to Damascus, Bogotá, Cairo, Moscow and Riyadh. On these journeys they traveled by commercial means, alone, and had to make contact with T.R.U.T.H. operatives already in-country. The only thing they did not practice was the actual taking of a human life. But they knew that too was coming.

Ned absorbed his learning like a thirsty man who had found an oasis in the desert. His physical development was so dramatic that he hardly recognized himself in the mirror. His waist size decreased by four inches, and his neck size increased by two. Mentally, he was instilled with a tough-ness that encountered each succeeding assignment with greater confidence.

Where he struggled was in the ethical realm. He had been a devout Christian since childhood. His relationship to God was very important to him, and it had carried him through many rough spots. Now his belief system was being challenged with ideas that called into question his view of the sacredness of life.

It was a problem he had to deal with alone. One evening he carefully broached the subject with Isaiah and Alpha. Their reaction told him that this was his issue and not theirs. Isaiah pressed him a bit, but he backed away from it and never mentioned it again.

As his training was nearing its end, every night he thought about the matter of assassination as he waited for sleep to come. One night he had another one of his colorful dreams. It was in a court room setting. Sitting on the bench was Almighty God. The prosecution table was very long. There were more than thirty prosecutors. The lead defense attorney was the current President of the United States. The jury consisted of every day people….men and women, black and white. He recognized one as a Jewish Rabbi, another as an Imam, and a third was the pastor of his childhood. Behind the defense table sat Brian, Kara and Anita Reed. Next to them were Cheryl and Grace.

All eyes were on the defendant, Ned Francis Reed.

The judge was addressing the jury. "Ladies and Gentlemen, have you reached a verdict?"

The forewoman, a kind, grandmotherly type, looked at the judge, and then at Ned.

"We find the defendant, the defendant, the defendant….."

Ned awoke, drenched in perspiration and breathing heavily. He turned on the lamp next to the bed. He took out a pad and pen. Across the top of the page he wrote two questions, drawing a line down the center between them. He wrote feverishly and when he was done, he read over his notes:

When is it justified to take a life?	When is it wrong to take another life?
In self-defense	In anger
To save other lives	For personal gain
To avert a disaster	Simply for ideological reasons
In defense of country	Out of revenge
To protect one's family	When offering your own life would have the same "positive" outcome

Comparing the lists, he reached two conclusions. First, that there *were* extenuating circumstances when another life may have to be sacrificed. And second, if called upon to do so, he would evaluate the motives in each instance. *Could my superiors live with that? Could I walk such a moral tightrope?*

His final thought before finally succumbing to sleep was, "God have mercy on us all!"

• •

The mid to late 1980's were a chaotic time. On the national scene, the future of space exploration was put in doubt as the country reeled from the Challenger disaster. Economic uncertainty gripped the nation after Black Monday hit Wall Street in the fall of '87. TV shows and movies continued to push the envelope in their ongoing commentary on American life and values.

As immigrants, some legal and some not, poured in from Central America, Asia and the Middle East, the U.S. melting pot began to boil. The actor, by the way, got four more years in the White House. And Ned's beloved New York Yankees vanished from the radar screen as year after year they sank deeper in the standings.

Chaos and change were not restricted to America. While entertainers sang, "We Are the World," that same world was becoming a more dangerous place. As Ned prepared to leave the nest at Quantico to enter the fray, the Iran-Contra Scandal made world headlines. A British journalist was kidnapped by the Islamic Jihad to begin five and one-half years in captivity...an omen of things to come.

The greatest nuclear disaster in history erupted in Chernobyl, contaminating the atmosphere of all of Northern Europe. Tensions in the Soviet Union were at an all-time high as hard-liners tried desperately to maintain their power against reformers, like Boris Yeltsin. And their army was being demoralized day after day in the mountains of Afghanistan.

In a few short years the wall would be down, McDonalds would open in Moscow, and the Cold war would end. But it was not over yet. The international climate was filled with intrigue. Agents of T.R.U.T.H. were being dispatched to every continent, gathering information and initiating covert activity to protect the nation and its people.

On to such a landscape came the agency's newest operative Ned Reed, code-named "Archangel." His first assignments brought him to Russia and some of the eastern-bloc nations. He posed at various times as a journalist, a scientist, and an arms dealer. Through some greedy bureaucrats and a few risky night missions he obtained valuable information which he passed on to his contacts in the States.

To his surprise it was nearly two years before he was directed to take a human life. On December 21, 1988, terrorism revealed its ugliness in the skies over Lockerbie, Scotland, when a Pan Am jet was turned into a fiery bomb. Two hundred seventy men, women and children lost their lives that day. Within hours it was ascertained that this had been the work of Islamic extremists from Libya. The world would not know this for many months.

Irrefutable evidence was also uncovered that a second such attack was planned for one week later, this time on an Air France Concorde leaving Orly airport bound for New York. The plot was discovered through a reliable informant and an apartment on the Left Bank in Paris was identified as the staging point. Two men, one from Libya and the other from Yemen, were being kept under constant surveillance.

Archangel's mission was straightforward. He was to eliminate the "combatants" and gather any evidence from the scene. In light of the imminent threat to innocent lives, Ned never questioned the justification for this action. Late one night he entered the apartment like a phantom and shot the terrorists in their sleep. He gathered whatever he could and was gone within minutes. And he didn't give it a second thought.

CHAPTER TWENTY-THREE

Kate Fowler and Mike McKenna sat across the kitchen table from Ned and Jill. A fresh pot of coffee sat on a trivet in the center of the table, its aroma filling the room.

"Before we begin," said Fowler, "Mike and I want you to know that we are among those from the Bureau assigned to a special task force under the Department of Homeland Security. Our mandate is to investigate and apprehend all individuals who represent a threat to our country. Jill, you may be a source for us since you knew your husband better than anyone. His travels and contacts have aroused the suspicion of many in our government."

"I had no idea."

"I guess we'll proceed under that assumption. But remember, your involvement in this is highly unusual. We ask you to participate only when specifically asked to do so."

Jill nodded. "OK, what's next?"

Putting his coffee mug down, McKenna took over. "We will interview you later in-depth about your marriage and your husband. Right now, we need the two of you to describe everything that occurred since your hasty departure from New York."

Once again, Ned and Jill went into great detail over events precipitated by David's Hovnanian's frantic phone call to his wife. The agents listened carefully, and Kate made occasional notes on a notepad. When Ned recounted his clandestine visit to David's office, the two of them looked at one another and smiled.

"It's a good thing Valone isn't here, Rich," said Mike. "We might have had to bail you out of jail. I'm beginning to see that we have a formidable ally, Kate."

Turning back to Ned, he continued. "I assume you have something to show us then."

Ned retrieved the copied ledger and the agents eagerly scanned it for a few minutes. He interrupted their concentration. "So do you want to know about my meeting with Andropov?"

Kate and Mike were suddenly speechless. He had their total attention. Jill stared at him too, her eyes wide in confusion, and fear.

"Before you two arrived on the scene, it was my plan to extricate Jill from this fox hunt. It took little time to figure out from that book that Sergei Andropov was probably in the middle of this mess. Through phone records I tracked him down in Coney Island, and confronted him. I can assure you that his interest in that little book is much greater than ours."

Jill reached over and grasped his arm. "They could have killed you?"

"It did get a little hairy for a while. But Andropov isn't going to harm either one of us as long as this book is safe. I'm supposed to contact him tomorrow evening to see if he's willing to live with this stand-off."

Kate reacted to this revelation. "You realize that we can't leave it at that. There are much bigger issues at stake. If this information could avert another terrorist attack, we have to follow it where it leads."

Taking Jill's hand, Ned said, "I understand what you're saying, but it's not up to me to gamble with this woman's life."

"Ned... er Rich. These people, whoever they are, can't be trusted. I feel like my life will always be at risk. I think the only way to be free is to put them out of business."

They were all silent for a time.

"All right," Ned said. "I have to make a couple of calls before I can commit myself to this, and I assume the two of you have to consult with your bosses. If we get that far, we have less than twenty-four hours to come up with a plan."

After agreeing to meet again later in the day, the agents left the apartment. What Ned hoped would be the end of this nightmare, seemed now to only be the beginning.

Leaving Jill in the kitchen, Ned went to his bedroom, took another cell phone from his night table, propped himself on the bed, and dialed a number in Northern Virginia. It was picked up on the second ring. A mechanical voice said just one word: "Identify." He punched in a series of numbers that he hadn't used in many months. He could hear his call then being transferred to another line. This time he heard a familiar human voice.

"We missed you, Archangel."

"I told you that I wouldn't call again until I was ready."

"We didn't think it would take this long. There were some here in the family who wanted to declare you compromised, a renegade. You know what has to be done with lost sheep."

"You know me better than that, Blanchard."

"I'm your biggest fan, Ned. I wouldn't let anything happen to you. Your call isn't a complete surprise, though. We have intercepted several inquiries about you the last couple of days. What's going on? Are you ready to defend the motherland again?"

Ned gave him an abbreviated version of events, ending with the current involvement of the F.B.I. and Homeland Security. He concluded with the proposal to work in concert to expose and diffuse the possible threat.

His boss was quick to respond. "We've been monitoring this situation for some time, Ned. It's not my call, but the fact that you're already on the scene will probably mean that you'll get the OK. I will call you back within the hour."

"I'll be waiting."

"Welcome back, Archangel."

Ned hung up without responding to this comment. He was not sure that he was *back*.

The second number he dialed was to a home in New Jersey. It was a call he had started to place many times in recent months. Several times his soul-searching had led him back to a nursery at Sibley Memorial Hospital in Washington, D.C. Kara picked up the phone just as the answering machine began its message. "Hold on," she shouted, as she shut it off.

"Hello, big sister."

"Ned! I can't believe it's you. We began to think the worst. It's never been so long."

"I'm OK, Kara, and it's been a long time for me too. I'll explain it to you sometime. How is everybody?"

"We are empty-nesters now, Ned. Gracie moved out after graduation this Spring. She's a beautiful, intelligent, caring young woman. And it looks like she's also found her 'Mr. Wonderful.'"

Ned choked up. "She's all grown up. I do feel bad that I missed her graduation."

"She missed you too."

"Kara, I'll never be able to repay you and Garrett for what you've done for her."

"That check for her tuition should take care of it," she replied playfully. "But you must know that we have been the ones who were blessed by that girl."

Ned hesitated and there was a moment of silence. "Kara, I'm going to ask you something. I may not have the right to ask it, and I will respect your answer, but please listen. If it's possible, I want to know Grace as my daughter, and her to know me as her father."

He held his breath, but his sister began to laugh. "Well, it's about time. Ned, Gracie has always known that she was adopted, a chosen one, we like to say. Maybe earlier this might have been difficult for her, but not now. Recently, when she and I were talking about her marrying Tim, she's been asking more about her background. What a great gift this would be for her. And won't she be surprised?"

Ned began to weep softly. She offered him soothing words, and before the end of their conversation she gave him Grace's cell phone number.

CHAPTER TWENTY-FOUR

The next morning Fowler and McKenna were at Ned's door before nine o'clock. With them was a short Asian man in his fifties. He wore frameless glasses, had thinning gray hair, and a youthful complexion. Kate made the introductions. The newcomer was another member of the terrorism task force by the name of Jacob Chacko. Ned figured him to be of either Indian or Pakistani descent. He was an employee of the Central Intelligence Agency.

Ned shook the man's hand and guided him and the others into the living room.

"Welcome to the party, Jacob. Times certainly have changed, haven't they? The F.B.I. and the C.I.A. on the same team?"

"It's a different world, Richard. And I understand that we don't even know who *you* are."

McKenna cleared his throat. "Its time, folks. Rich, are you in or not?"

"Full- speed ahead."

"That's good because we hope that you will be the kingpin of this operation. Our analysts have been at work all night accessing additional data and attempting to decipher the ledger. At this point we think we understand enough to know that we have to act quickly to eliminate a legitimate threat."

"This is starting to sound like a spy thriller," Jill remarked. McKenna ignored her comment. "We are aware of some of the names listed. Knowing their previous activities, as well as Hovnanian's itinerary the past several months, we are suggesting that he has been arranging a deal to make nuclear material from the old Soviet Union available to interested parties in the Middle East. It appears that this is being brokered somehow by the Russian mob in this country.

"Andropov."

"Yes, Sergei Andropov. He was a neighborhood bully on the streets of Moscow, and has now transformed himself into some kind of Godfather since moving to the States. We don't believe this deal has gone down yet, and has probably been delayed by Hovnanian's skimming, and his subsequent murder. That's where you come in, Richard."

"What are you proposing, Mike?"

"We want you to go back to Andropov and look for a piece of the action."

Jill was on her feet. "That's crazy! There's already been one murder."

Again the agent proceeded as if she were not even in the room. "Meet him in a public place. Offer to seal the deal for a handsome price. These people don't want to get directly involved in this stuff. They just want their millions with which to finance other criminal enterprises. What do you think?"

"Andropov is no fool, but I suppose I am the only one with access to him. I can give it a shot. It will have to be a perfect con. Let me suggest how we might do this."

It took another half-hour to come up with a plausible cover story. Then Ned dialed the number of the Russian club. Andropov answered it himself.

"Sergei, the rules have changed. Meet me at the Nathan's in Times Square this afternoon at five o'clock. Come alone."

"Who are you to tell me what to do?"

"I am your knight in shining armor, my friend. Be there at five." Ned immediately hung up the phone.

CHAPTER TWENTY-FIVE

Ned glanced at his watch. It was almost ten at night and he debated whether it was too late to call his daughter. He knew that he wouldn't sleep unless he at least tried. He thought for a moment what he might say, composed himself, and dialed.

"Hello."

He almost hung up and his mouth went dry. "Hi, Grace."

"Uncle Ned? I've been waiting to hear that voice again. We have all been worried sick about you."

"I know Gracie. I talked with your mom already. I'm sorry for upsetting you all."

"Uncle Ned, I have so many wonderful things to tell you. When can I see you?

She's making this easy for me. "Honey, I know this is short notice, but is there any way we can have lunch tomorrow. I'm here in New York, and I see from your area code that you're here too."

"I'd love it. I live on the Lower East Side with a couple of roommates, but I work near the financial district. If you could meet me down there, I'm sure I can get permission for an extended lunch hour."

"That would be great. Do you know a place called Renaldo's? It's just off of Maiden Lane."

"You bet. I've been there a couple of times."

"How about 11:30?"

"I can't wait to see my favorite uncle."

You should only know, child. "I'll be there."

When Ned came out of the bedroom Jill was reading a recent issue of Time magazine. She looked up and immediately saw the expression on his face. "What happened to you?"

He gave her a weary smile. "It's too complicated to explain right now, Jill. Let's just say I feel about twenty-three years old again."

CHAPTER TWENTY-SIX

The failure and fall of Soviet-style communism, symbolized on every television screen by the dismantling of the Berlin Wall, signaled for many the end of the Cold War, and a new era of peace and cooperation.

There was no celebration in a non-descript office on a busy commercial strip in Arlington, Virginia. The lettering in the front window identified it as "Jonas Faulk and Associates, Certified Public Accountants." There was actually a receptionist/secretary and two CPAs who carried on a moderately successful business. Three other offices with nameplates sat vacant. The last door near the rear of the building was marked "Employees Only." It led to a staircase which was accessible by punching in a numerical code on an electronic touch pad. An identical lock led to the same stairway from the alley which ran the entire block behind the complex.

This was the Operations Center for the Tactical Response Unit for the Homeland. It was run by just three individuals who were surrounded by the most sophisticated electronic devices ever assembled in one place.

T.R.U.T.H. had long anticipated the end of the Cold war, and was acutely aware of the dangers it presented. They knew that the entire Soviet nuclear arsenal, spread across the eastern bloc, would now be largely unprotected. Rogue states would be jockeying for position, as the world's balance of power shifted. Saddam Hussein wasted no time in testing the will of the West by invading Kuwait, igniting the Gulf War and Operation Desert Storm.

Islamic terrorist groups were emboldened to flex their muscles in the Middle East and elsewhere, even in the U.S. A carefully planned truck bombing in the basement of the World Trade Center in New York caused severe damage and much panic. In the Middle East itself, tensions between Palestinians and Jews exploded time and again. Hezbullah and Hamas arose to press Yasser Arafat's PLO toward greater militancy.

It was in such a political and ideological climate that Ned Reed, A.K.A. Archangel, operated throughout the '90's. He personally played a role in several world events, though his name and face never appeared in any headline. His travels took him all over the world. In late 1994 he made a twelve hour visit to Rwanda. That day the mysterious deaths of two Hutu leaders hastened the end to the genocide there. Months before NATO attacked Serbia in the former Yugoslavia in 1999, Archangel was there, stealing high level communiqués exposing Serbia's intent to eradicate all Ethnic Albanians.

Nine-Eleven changed everyone's world. 2001 had not been lacking in global unrest. There was a major escalation of suicide bombings in the Holy Land. Political assassinations in Africa only complicated the latest round of drought and starvation. AIDS swept across the continent like an uncontrollable wild fire. And in the States people were reminded that the Cold war had not fully thawed when F.B.I. agent Robert Hansen was arrested for spying for Russia.

Everyone remembers where they were at 8:14 am, Eastern Daylight Time, on September 11, 2001. Ned Reed was in a hotel room in Bogotá, Columbia. He was awaiting instructions for an operation against the Cali drug cartel. CNN was on in the background as he reviewed documents which he had brought with him. The news bulletin and ensuing footage mesmerized him. He knew that his current assignment would be cancelled. With much of the rest of the world he watched hour after hour as the drama in New York unfolded. Over and over again they replayed the plane strikes and the collapsing of the towers.

America agonized in shock and disbelief. What held Archangel's attention were the people in capitol cities all over the Arab world, dancing in the streets.

CHAPTER TWENTY-SEVEN

By the time the government agents concluded their strategy session with Ned and Jill, it was ten past eleven in the morning. Grabbing a light jacket from the hall closet, Ned turned to her.

"I have to go out for a couple of hours. Help yourself to some lunch."

"Let me go with you. I'm beginning to feel these walls closing in on me."

"I have to do this alone, Jill. But if all goes well, later today I'll take you out for a fancy dinner."

He quickly left the apartment after reminding her to set the locks. He caught up with Fowler, McKenna, and Chacko just as they were getting into a government-issued, black Crown Victoria, which had been parked illegally out in front.

"Can I hitch a ride? I'm supposed to be all the way downtown in less than twenty minutes."

Kate raised an eyebrow. "Where are you going now, mystery man?"

"Don't worry, this is strictly personal."

Midday traffic in Lower Manhattan can be a nightmare, but they were able to get within two blocks of Ned's destination before being trapped in gridlock. It was close enough for him. He bid them farewell and then disappeared on the crowded sidewalk. It was about 11:40 when he entered Renaldo's.

The noise of the city was hushed as soon as the door closed behind him. His eyes adjusted to the dimly lit dining room and spotted Grace at a table-for-two in a far corner. She was sipping some kind of drink. By the time he reached the table she was out of her seat. She put her arms around his waist and squeezed tightly. He kissed her on the top of her head and held her. He was afraid to let go.

"Oh, it's so good to see you, Uncle Ned. I've missed you so much."

"Gracie. Let's sit down and order. We have a lot of catching up to do. What are you drinking?"

Grace smiled broadly. "It's just some iced tea. Did you think it was something stronger? I'm legal now you know, but alcohol is an acquired taste, which I haven't acquired yet."

"Good. It seems to be something that gets a lot of people into trouble."

"You sound just like my father, but then I guess that's not a bad thing. Daddies are protective of their little girls."

Ned nearly choked on the water he had just sipped. He had to change the subject.

"So what's been happening in your life? Your mom told me a little, but I want to hear it all from you."

"The big news is that I'm in love. Tim…I must have mentioned him before. Well, we have been dating for almost two years. He proposed to me on graduation night."

"You're really sure about this guy?" *So this is what a father feels.*

"I've never been surer of anything. I can't wait for you to meet him."

"I guess everything else is old news then, Grace."

"Well, let's see. I did manage to get my degree in Communications from N.Y.U."

"I'm sorry I missed the celebration."

"I understand. Over the years you've had to be gone a lot. I'm glad you're here, right now."

Ned couldn't wait any longer. He could hardly breathe. "Gracie, there's a special reason I wanted to see you today. Your mom mentioned to me that you've been asking about your birth-parents."

"Uncle Ned, I realized that I know so little about my history. When Tim and I have kids, I feel like I should know if there are any medical issues."

Here goes. "I think I can help you with that, sweetheart."

Ned took out his wallet and removed an old photo, taken on the boardwalk at Rehobeth Beach. Two newlyweds had big smiles for the camera. The picture was laminated to protect it from the elements. He handed it to his daughter.

Gracie's hand trembled as she took the snapshot from him. She stared at it for a long time. Tears began to dampen her cheeks. Finally, she whispered, "I look just like her."

Ned was stunned by her reaction. "You act like you already knew."

"I've thought long and hard throughout my life about who my real parents were. I can't explain it, but I pictured my father just like you. I've almost wished that it were so. There's always a been chemistry between us. And there have been certain non-verbal things between mom and you, when it came to me. I almost came right out and asked her recently, but then I 'chickened-out.'"

"Amazing. I thought that you would be upset and angry."

"I don't know exactly what I feel right now. I do know that you have a lot of explaining to do, Unc....*she laughed nervously*....do I call you father?"

And so Ned told her everything about Cheryl, their courtship, their short but happy marriage, and finally about the tragic night that changed both his and Grace's life.

"Did she suffer a lot?"

"She never regained consciousness. It was a miracle that you survived. It was only by the grace of God that you were born. That's why I named you Grace."

Ned could sense the mood shifting. *Maybe she does know what she's feeling?* He saw pain in her eyes.

"You gave me up. Why?"

"I don't expect you to understand, Grace. I have asked the same question a thousand times. All I can say is that at the time I was a totally empty man. I felt I had nothing to offer you but sadness and struggle. Your mom and dad agreed to love you as their own. And I think they did quite a job."

"Yes they have! I guess I have to face the fact that I have two dads now."

"Garrett is your dad, Gracie. If I can have a place in your life I will be grateful. I will love you always no matter what you decide to do about me."

Grace's face softened. She rose, came across the table and sat on Ned's lap, burying her face in his chest. Unaware of what was really occurring, all eyes in Renaldo's were drawn to this pair.

The tension dissipated and the rest of the lunch was more light-hearted. Grace had a giggling fit when she realized that her brothers and sisters were also her cousins, her mom and dad were her aunt and uncle, and that she had a living grandmother who she had never met.

It had gone better than Ned could have imagined. This wonderful young woman was his girl, and they would have a new relationship. When they hugged outside the restaurant and headed their separate ways, Ned raised his face heavenward. "Thank you, Lord. Now make me the father and the man you want me to be."

In his exuberance the usually vigilant Archangel did not notice a scruffy looking man turning the next corner, about twenty paces behind Grace.

CHAPTER TWENTY-EIGHT

Following the numbing tragedy in New York, T.R.U.T.H and all of its known counterparts in the U.S. Intelligence Community, were enlisted in the war against terror. Almost all world events were now viewed against the backdrop of terrorism. Regimes were deemed either for or against us in the fight. The interdiction of drugs was now seen as a way to combat the financing of terrorist activities. The invasion of Afghanistan revealed the tip of the proverbial iceberg in the proliferation of terrorist training camps.

A folk hero emerged in the person of Osama bin Laden, who blatantly fueled the frenzy of hatred toward non-Muslims and anything Western. "Al Quada" became a household word, representing a loosely knit, but highly dangerous network of cells operating around the world.

This was a new kind of war. Mighty armies and arsenals were seemingly helpless against invisible foes who could strike at will. Young men and women were lining up to be strapped with suicide bombs in order to be martyrs for the cause. Paradise and rewards were promised them, while their leaders plotted from the safety of their strongholds.

The least public but most effective methods to combat terrorism were carried out by the clandestine agents of the Tactical Response Unit for The Homeland. For years they had moved quietly in and out of various cultures, influencing or silencing enemies of freedom. In the thirty years of its existence, it had rarely failed a mission and never lost an agent.

The years prior to 9/11 provided Ned with a steady stream of assignments across the globe. He was paid handsomely after each mission. His name appeared on no government payroll and he paid no taxes. After that fateful day, he was barraged by work which afforded little time for reconnaissance and preparation. He lived in constant danger of detection, and had to rely on his well-honed instincts more than he would have wished.

He was in Afghanistan prior to the invasion against the Taliban. He was in Iraq weeks before the second Gulf war and provided crucial information to the military. His flawless linguistic skills and mastery of disguises allowed him to move almost at will around the Middle East. But he was ever aware that a single slip could end his career and his life.

In early 2002, he was sent to Israel where fourteen suicide attacks had killed dozens and wounded hundreds of others. He was able to identify a specific faction within Hamas which was behind the killings. This was relayed through T.R.U.T.H. to Israeli Intelligence. A subsequent raid on a safe house in Gaza quelled the attacks, at least for a time. The following year Ned arrived in Saudi Arabia a day late, after thirty-four were killed in a western compound there. Intelligence agencies were just not able to keep up with suspected threats. He was reassigned to view the aftermath, and propose ways of beefing up security in the area. His cover was that of an envoy from the Secretary General of the United Nations. By the time the real U.N. observers were on the scene, he was already gone.

The election of a new hard-liner as President of Iran, a man who touted himself as an instrument of Allah in the fight against Israel and the West, now destabilized the region further. He pursued his nuclear aspirations in the face of protest from many quarters. Ned spent much time in Teheran and other cities, encouraging opposition groups. On more than one occasion he escaped just minutes before government agents raided his location.

Archangel's last assignment before his retreat to San Marcos was in Russia, where he had spent much of his time prior to the fall of Soviet Communism. He was surprised to find that despite the appearance of free elections and inroads of capitalism in the economy, cronyism and old party bonds were turning Mother Russia back toward the rule of the few. But this was the concern of diplomats. Ned's work was much more concrete. Ironically, his final assignment was to stop the hemorrhaging of nuclear technology and materials from behind the old Iron Curtain. In two short weeks, he eliminated the three top exporters of such material and sent the market in such commodities into chaos. It would not be long before they would regroup.

CHAPTER TWENTY-NINE

N ed came out of the subway at Forty-Third Street and Broadway a few minutes before five. The sidewalks were packed with natives and tourists. Approaching Nathan's slowly, he immediately spotted two of Andropov's cronies from the social club. One was wearing a blue uniform and was washing the windows of the restaurant with a bucket of suds and a long-handled squeegee. The second man was standing outside the place handing out leaflets to whoever would take them. Ned took one as he reached for the door. It was a coupon for a massage parlor somewhere in the area.

Andropov was sitting in a booth by himself sipping a soft drink. Ned slid in across from him. He addressed him in Russian. "Have you tried a hotdog, Sergei. Nathan's makes the best in the world."

"You want to talk to me? So, talk!"

"I told you to come alone."

"I am alone."

"You could have let Moe and Curly come in from the outside."

"Never mind them. I am here. You have five minutes, and the clock is running."

"Not here, Andropov. I want you to follow me next door. Your men can go with us."

The Russian followed Ned out the door and nodded to his comrades who fell in line behind them. They rounded the corner and entered a building that was undergoing renovations. The workers had left for the day, but the front door was open. They went to an office in the rear on the first floor. There were several folding chairs scattered around the room. Judging from the refuse strewn about, it was probably the place where the construction workers ate their lunches.

It was now or never....time for the big con. Ned had rehearsed this in his mind all afternoon. He picked up the conversation, again in fluent Russian.

"OK, here's the deal. The ledger will stay in a safe place. It is our insurance policy. As long as Mrs. Hovnanian and I are safe, you have nothing to fear. But Sergei, I have been doing a little studying of the material. I think I know what Hovnanian was doing for you. He just got a little greedy. I figure you need someone to finish the job."

"You have no idea, Mr. Henry, what this is about."

"Just listen and you can tell me if I'm wrong. I think David Hovnanian was your point man, arranging for the sale of radioactive material from persons in the former Soviet Union to interested parties in the Muslim world. How am I doing, Sergei?"

Andropov was pensive, studying Ned's face. Finally he spoke. "Who are you and who do you work for?"

The Russian was examining the bait. "Actually I used to work for the U.S. Government, and at a different time you might have been on my target list. But that was a long time ago. I got sick of doing other peoples' dirty work so that one day I could get a gold-watch and a little pension. Now I work for myself and I have become a wealthy man. I have come to like my lifestyle, Sergei, but I am not a greedy man. We could arrive at a reasonable figure and then I will deliver for you."

"How do I know I can trust you?"

"I don't expect you to trust me anymore than I trust you. But that doesn't mean we can't do business."

Suddenly Andropov reached into his pocket, pulled out a twenty-five caliber pistol and tossed it to Ned. Pointing to the man in the blue uniform he said, "Kill him!"

In one motion Ned brought the weapon up and aimed it at the forehead of the man he had nicknamed "Moe." When he looked into his eyes he froze. Five seconds can seem an eternity to someone drawn into a life and death decision. *I don't know anything about this man. Does he deserve to die?*

The decision was wrenched from him. The gun had a hair-trigger which yielded to the slightest pressure. It exploded in his hand. The man, who had been standing near the doorway, collapsed in a heap. His death was instantaneous.

"Call me at eight in the morning," Andropov said. He left the room with his remaining escort, leaving Ned and the corpse behind.

Archangel stared first at the empty doorway and then at the dead man. In that moment all of his life energy seemed to drain from him. He looked at his hand, still holding the gun, and it began to tremble. He threw it aside, dropped to his knees and vomited. Gazing again at the lifeless body of his adversary, he began to weep. *What's wrong with me?*

He was changing. He had killed many people without a shred of guilt. Now the lines he had so clearly defined were blurring. He realized that he didn't want to take another human life again....ever....for any reason.

****

When he finally left the building the sun was consider-ably lower in the sky and was hidden behind the skyscrapers to the west. It felt like the temperature had dropped ten degrees. Ned joined the thinning crowds and made his way back to the subway entrance. He walked through the maze below the city and then reappeared on Broadway at another subway exit.

Before his eyes could adjust to the light, the Crown Vic pulled up to the curb and the rear door swung open. He settled in the seat as the light turned green and they proceeded south. The F.B.I. agents were in the front seat and Chacko sat next to Ned. He was the first to speak.

"What happened?"

By now Archangel had composed himself. "We're in."

Fowler leaned back and spoke next. "We saw four of you go in and only two leave. We were wondering if they left one behind to dispose of you."

"I'm afraid it was the other way around, Kate. I had to prove my loyalty. Andropov had me kill one of his own guys."

"What a savage. Should we have someone go back and clean up the carnage?"

Ned was emphatic. "No! That would be the civilized thing to do, but we don't want to draw any more attention. They may go back for him themselves or just leave him for the workers to find tomorrow."

"What now?" said McKenna.

"Nothing until morning. Andropov could change his mind. I don't ever want to trust that man."

They lapsed into silence unto they pulled up to Ned's apartment house. Mike switched off the engine. They all reached for the door handles but Ned stopped them. "That's it for tonight, folks."

Chacko objected. "But we have a lot of planning to do."

"No we don't. I have a date with a pretty woman for dinner. And then I have to do some thinking on my own. I don't know how to tell you this, but this has now become *my* operation."

"You must be kidding. You can't just dismiss the C.I.A. and the F.B.I. from this."

All eyes were now on Ned. He took a deep breath. "You people know very little about me except that we seem to be on the same side. Well, I have to tell you that I work alone. If I need your support, I'll ask for it."

Fowler was livid. "There is too much at stake here. You just can't play Lone Ranger, Rich. Our superiors won't even consider it."

"You don't understand. The more bureaucracy is involved, the lower the chances will be of success. You will be brought in when it's time to round up the bad guys."

McKenna was already on his cell phone. Ned nodded to Chacko. "Jacob, you should be making a call too. Tell them to check with the same source that OK'd me yesterday."

Within ten minutes the agents had received word back that they should defer to Ned's instructions. They were not happy.

Fowler shook her head. "I hope you know what you're doing, Mr. Super Hero. I can't believe that they're willing to let you do this alone."

"I understand your concern, I really do. It's not that I don't appreciate what you can do. I'm sure I'll need your help at some point."

"What are you going to do with Andropov?"

"If I tell you, I'd have to kill you," Ned said with a smile. "I'll tell you what. I will contact you at prearranged times so that you will know that I'm still in the game. If there's anything to know or do I'll tell you along the way. That's the best that I can do."

With that he opened the car door and moved out on to the sidewalk. Leaning back, he smiled. "You must excuse me. It's never good to keep a lady waiting."

Jill had seen the car arrive and waited impatiently by the window while the four of them negotiated. She had the door open before he could reach the handle. She threw her arms around him. "I was terrified that I wouldn't see you again."

"What a nice welcome home."

"I have a hundred questions," she said excitedly.

"The only question I'm prepared to answer is where we are going to eat. I am a man of his word, and we are going to have a nice dinner together."

They both showered and dressed, and left the house just before eight. They walked hand-in-hand for a couple of blocks to an avenue lined with commercial establishments. Small cafes and bistros beckoned to diners with their memo boards on the sidewalk. Many of them had strands of small lights adorning their porticos.

They went straight to the next corner where Ned directed Jill down a flight of stairs to a plain entranceway. Over the door was a small sign: "Le Bon Vie."

To her surprise they entered an elegant dining room. Every table but one was occupied, and waiters moved unobtrusively between them. The maitre de nodded to Ned and seated them at the remaining table.

"*Bon soir, Monsieur* Carlson."

"*Merci beaucoup*, Claude. Thank you for making room for us tonight."

"There will always be room for you, *mon ami*."

When he left and they were alone Jill began to giggle

"What's so funny?"

"Being with you is an adventure, *mon ami*."

"At your service, *madame*. I hope you like French cuisine."

They ordered escargot as an appetizer, and finished a loaf of warm bread even before their salads arrived. They decided on Chateaubriand for the main course, and also shared a bottle of light wine. They spoke little as they savored the small but succulent portions of food.

After ordering *crème brulee* and coffee, they looked at one another in the glow of candlelight. They were totally relaxed. Jill spoke softly. "I know I should be grieving the loss of a husband and worrying about the future, but I am so glad to be right here with you, Ned."

"Are you sure it's not the wine?"

She took his hand in hers. "I do want to know who you are. You are a good person, a moral person. You have risked your life for me. You seem to be a man with many secrets. I may not have the right to know them, Ned, but I won't betray your trust."

"It seems to be easier to risk my life than to reveal myself, Jill. That goes a long way back. But I'm tired of keeping secrets, and I'm tired of being alone. You must believe me when I tell you that you wouldn't want to know the details of the last twenty years of my life. I believed that I was making the world a better and a safer place. I still think that was true, but I'm not sure if I want to be that person anymore."

He took a sip of water and continued. "I killed a man today. I have done it many times before. But today it made me sick, literally and figuratively. I went to San Marcos to find myself again, Jill. It didn't happen in seven months. And then you came along. I know now that I can't go back to the old way of life, but I have to settle this one last assignment. I have to do it for you, and for me."

She had never let go of his hand. Now she reached across and stroked his cheek. She summoned up the courage to ask, "Has there ever been a woman in this life of yours?"

"There have been two. One was my soul-mate. We were planning to grow old together but more than twenty years ago she was taken from me by a drunken driver. I realized only today that I have been holding on to my grief to somehow preserve my relationship with her. Pretty sick, huh?"

Jill's eyes were filled with tears. "Sick? No, but very sad. What about the second woman?"

"I had lunch with her today. She is a bright, vivacious young woman who looks remarkably like her mother...the mother she never knew."

"You have a daughter?"

"Yes, but she didn't know her father until today."

"Wow."

"She has been raised by my sister and brother-in-law as their own. And they did a great job. But this new me couldn't be a spectator any longer."

"Was she angry with you?"

"Maybe a little. I'm not sure she knows what to feel. It may take some time, but if today was any indication, I think I'm going to have a daughter in my life from now on."

They finished their desserts and Ned paid the bill. He left a generous tip for the wait staff which had seemed to sense when to interrupt and when to leave them alone. Back on the sidewalk, Jill reached up and kissed him. "Thank you," she said.

"It *is* one of my favorite places to eat."

"Not for the dinner, dummy. Thanks for sharing you."

They began to walk, but he wasn't finished. "Jill, it is weird. I haven't felt this vulnerable since I was a kid, but I don't even care. I can't help but feel that God has something really important for me to do with the rest of my life. I just have to discover what it is."

"You are really serious about this God stuff, aren't you? You *do* go to church on Sundays."

"Without God, nothing makes sense." He looked directly at her. "Does it scare you when I talk like that?"

"You don't scare me at all, Ned Reed. And neither does your God."

CHAPTER THIRTY

His dinner with Jill was everything he wanted it to be. It was well past mid-night when Ned's mind quieted down, enabling him to fall asleep. He began to dream immediately. He had been on a long journey through desolate terrain. Tired and hungry, he peered into the distance. Above a hill he saw a plume of smoke. Staggering to the crest of the hill, he saw a fertile valley below. Small farms dotted the landscape. Row after row of hearty crops sat waiting to be harvested. In a far schoolyard, hundreds of children were playing.

The smoke he had seen was coming from a white clapboard house perched on the side of the hill. He climbed down into the yard and ascended the steps. In front of the door was a huge mat with one word on it: "Home." Peeking through the narrow window next to the door, he saw a warm and inviting great room. When he knocked, the door opened on its own. Across the room a fire crackled in the hearth and there was soft music playing in the background. He stepped into the room.

He was startled by a voice from the next room. "Honey, is that you?" It was Cheryl's voice. She came through the doorway and Ned caught her in a deep embrace. When she finally pulled away, Ned was gazing into the eyes of Jill Hovnanian.

She spoke with Cheryl's voice. "I was terrified that I might not ever see you again."

He was speechless, but then began to laugh. He laughed so hard and so long that his laughter turned to tears. He couldn't stop.

"Ned, Ned. It's all right. I'm here with you."

He forced his eyes open. Jill was holding him. "You must have been having a nightmare."

He smiled weakly. "It wasn't a nightmare, Jill. But I'm glad you're here."

• •

When he awoke, light was just beginning to filter through the bedroom curtains. Jill was sleeping soundly as he passed her room. He went to the kitchen where he filled the coffee maker and switched it on. The digital clock on the microwave told him it was 6:45. He had only a little more than an hour to consider how he would handle Andropov. This was the first opportunity for him to be totally alone since he left the Island. He remembered those quiet mornings of reflection on San Marcos, and decided that the Russian could wait.

He opened his laptop and began to write down his thoughts and feelings as he had on each of those tropical mornings. His fingers moved over the keys for thirty minutes. When he finished, he began rereading what he had journaled.

"I am a man who is full of contradictions. My life feels out of control, but full of excitement at the same time. I feel like a toddler learning how to walk again. But like a toddler I am curious about what is just out of my grasp.

Oh, God, what is to become of me?

Cheryl! I am not your husband anymore. You released me long ago, but I've kept you a prisoner in my soul. Forgive me?

Jill! What am I to do with you? Are we just two needy persons who have met by chance, and are using one another? By chance? I don't think so. I stopped believing in coincidence a long time ago. Trust your instincts, Ned. Listen to your heart for a change.

Grace! I don't deserve this chance she's giving me. Lord, don't let me blow it."

A soft voice interrupted his reading. It was not Cheryl, but Jill. "What are you doing, big guy?"

He turned and faced her. She was standing in the kitchen in her nightshirt. Her eyes had not fully opened, and her hair seemed to be pointing in all directions.

"You startled me," he said.

"I do look a little frightful in the morning, don't I?"

"Not this morning, Jill. Not this morning."

• •

With a calm resolve Ned dialed the number of the Russian club in Brooklyn. It was nearly 9:00. Andropov answered. "You're late."

"I've had a lot of preparations to make comrade. Are you ready to do business?"

"I am not your comrade, Mr. Henry, or Carlson, and I think it would be in our mutual interest to make plans together from now on. Now, I have no desire to discuss this over the phone. Meet me near the entrance to Sunset Park in one hour." The line went dead.

Ned had to take a cab to make it in time. They found a bench and Andropov spoke immediately. "Enough posturing! What are you proposing?"

"First, I want to know why you are not brokering this deal yourself. Why pay me or someone else to do it?"

"This is simpler than you might imagine. We are strictly businessmen with no political agenda. This is a one-time deal from which we plan to walk away very wealthy. We want nothing leading back to us. Through means which you don't need to know, we have obtained the contacts on both sides of this. We have no personal connection to them. Mr. Hovnanian could have still been alive today if he hadn't betrayed us. The parties are still waiting for final arrangements to be made. They are no doubt nervous over the delay. Your job is to calm their fears and consummate the deal."

"And for this I will receive…?

"Five percent of the proceeds. That would be half a million dollars deposited wherever you wish."

"Let me get this straight. I take all the risks and you go off into the sunset with ten million dollars?"

"It would seem very generous for perhaps one week's labors."

"A realtor gets more of a cut for selling a house. I was thinking more along the lines of fifteen percent. I won't ask you what you offered Hovnanian."

"You will get the ten percent we offered him and not a penny more. But if you betray us, nothing will protect you and Mrs. Hovnanian. Not even a little black book. Do you understand?"

Ned smiled. "Sergei, I'm not a selfish man. When this is over, Mrs. Hovnanian and I will disappear. Perhaps we'll return to a deserted isle somewhere."

Andropov searched Ned's face for any sign of deceit. Ned knew what he was doing, and how to respond. He had been told by a double agent once that he should have been a poker player.

Finally, the Russian broke his stare. "OK, Mr. Richard Carlson, private investigator, it seems that we have an agreement. You have ten days to complete the transfer of goods and funds. I will give you the names of contacts in Moscow and Cairo. Failure is not an option, is that clear?"

"More than clear," Ned responded in Russian.

The Russian handed him an envelope and gave one last instruction. "I will expect a call from you each day at five in the afternoon, New York time." With that, he left the park, never looking back at his new business partner.

Archangel sat for a while on the bench. Then he too exited the park, but instead of heading toward the nearest subway station, he began walking briskly toward Downtown Brooklyn. In the distance he could see his objective, the Brooklyn Bridge. By the time he reached the walkway to cross the East River, his mind was clear and focused. He was ready again, at least one last time, to do battle with the forces of evil. On the Manhattan side he hailed a "gypsy" cab and went home.

As the taxi arrived at his place, Ned was preparing to dial Special Agent Kate Fowler on his cell phone. But spotting the familiar Crown Vic across the street, he pocketed his phone, crossed over and got into the passenger seat. Agent Mike McKenna sat behind the wheel.

"Good morning, Mike. What brings you to my side of town?"

"It wasn't my idea, Richard. I guess my bosses are a little antsy about this whole setup. I'm supposed to keep an eye on you."

"This is not acceptable, my friend. Sitting out here you're a poster boy for the Bureau. I don't want or need this kind of attention. I told you that I would call in. I was just about to do so when I saw you sitting here."

"McKenna handed Ned his cell phone. It was already connecting to the New York Field Office of the F.B.I. "Ask for Agent Ralston."

When Ned concluded the conversation he handed the phone back to Mike. "Baby-sitting time is over. Go get yourself a donut. I'll be in touch."

CHAPTER THIRTY-ONE

Following his final Russian operation Archangel was incommunicado for almost two weeks. He had never been out of contact with his T.R.U.T.H. superiors for that length of time. In fact, they were so concerned that they sent another agent from nearby Kasikstan to Kiev and then on to Moscow to search for him. They feared that he might have been uncovered and paid the ultimate price. It was not like Ned to drop out of sight. The man looking for him was a long-time friend. They had joined the agency less than a year apart, and would share a meal in Georgetown from time to time.

Ned was very much alive. Always the consummate professional, it had taken him less than a month to seek out and dismantle the whole nuclear-trafficking network. Miraculously he had moved in and around the Russian underworld at will, following a trail to the leaders of the operation.

What no one knew was that for almost a year Ned was experiencing periods of depression for weeks at a time. Throughout his career he had been self-assured and focused. His most recent work left him drained and uncertain about his desire to continue as an agent. He knew also that such a mind-set would put him at greater risk in future assignments.

For twelve days Archangel occupied a hotel room in a run-down section of the Russian capitol. He left the room only briefly for an occasional meal. He stopped shaving and slept much of the time. He spoke to no one.

In the meantime, Clyde Summers, A.K.A. "Pacman", was running down leads in pursuit of Ned. His well-tuned instincts eventually led him to a smelly hallway outside a peeling hotel door. His knock brought Ned to his feet. Adrenaline shot through Archangel's body. He called out in Russian, "Who is it?"

"Open the door, cowboy!"

He knew the voice instantly. Opening the door he looked into the face of his friend. "I wondered who they'd send to find me."

Stepping into the room, Clyde gave Ned an affectionate punch in the shoulder. "I just happened to be in the neighborhood. "*Que pasa, amigo*? Mother has been very worried about you."

"I'm sure she has. I'll bet she's been wondering if I had become the first rogue in the history of the agency."

"They know you too well, Ned. They were more concerned that you might be in a shallow grave somewhere."

"I'm glad it's you, Pacman. You're a good listener, and I think that's what I need right now. There's a greasy spoon around the corner. Care to share a bite?"

"How can I refuse such an offer?" But first, I need to call Mother.

Later they were stirring their soup. Clyde was patient, waiting for his friend to begin.

"Thank you for coming, buddy. It wasn't my intent to alarm the troops. It just kind of happened. I've been in a state of paralysis the last two weeks."

"That doesn't sound like you."

"I haven't been myself for a while. I can't put my finger on what's wrong. After the last several assignments I've gone into a funk. This one is the worst. I wonder if I'm losing it, Clyde."

"Mother knows some good shrinks."

"I don't know."

"Ned, how's your love life?"

"What?"

"All work and no play, my boy. As far as I know, you've been all work since the day I met you. Maybe it's time to play. When was your last vacation?"

"You know, Pac. We sometimes have weeks between jobs."

"That's not what I asked, man. I'm not talking about painting the house. Maybe it's time for a real break. And when did you take a vow of celibacy, Ned. Was it after you lost Cheryl?"

"I thought you were supposed to just listen. You're giving me more to brood about."

"Maybe it's time to get away. What's the worst thing that could happen?"

"I don't know."

"Listen to me. I'll cover this with the agency. I'll tell them that you are certifiably sane and that you just need a little quality time off. Don't come back until you're ready."

"I wouldn't know where to go."

Pacman broke into a big smile. "This is your lucky day, Archangel. I know where you can go, and no one will know where you are but me... not even Mother."

"I feel like I'd be running away, Clyde. How is that facing things?"

"Maybe it's your turn to run *toward* something, my friend....something new. What have you possibly got to lose?"

Pacman left late that night, and Ned sensed his mood beginning to lift. He went to bed with just one question on his mind. *"Where on earth is San Marcos?"*

CHAPTER THIRTY-TWO

Jill was sitting at the kitchen table munching on a ham sandwich. A newly opened bag of potato chips rested next to her plate. When Ned sat down across from her, she tossed him the bag of chips.

"I didn't know when you'd be back so I made a sandwich. Can I make one for you?"

"Thanks, but no. Eat your lunch."

She couldn't contain her curiosity any longer. "Well, what happened?"

"Jill, if all goes well, maybe this will be all over in a week or two. And should we decide to stiff the U.S. Government and its agencies, we could be quite wealthy."

"I don't...."

"I'm kidding. We'd be running for the rest of our lives."

"It's been less than a week and I feel like I've been running for a year, Ned. No thanks."

He put his hand over his heart. "Besides, we're with the good guys. Why be filthy rich when we can be true patriots and have the gratitude of the entire nation?"

"I just want to become a 'nobody' again."

"That sounds good to me. We'll let Fowler and McKenna take credit. Or maybe Larry King, or Geraldo Rivera."

He hesitated a moment. "I have to do a lot of traveling now, Jill. It's the only way to get this done."

"Take me with you, please."

"I'm sorry but I can't. It will be tricky enough on my own. You would be a distraction. A nice one, mind you, but still a distraction. There's no room for negotiation on this, Jill."

"I thought that's what you'd say. But you can't blame me for trying. I'm feeling like a prisoner. I don't like the soaps and I can't stand by for the local weather on the 8's all day."

Ned took her hand. "I know this is no fun for you, but this is the way it has to be. When the time comes, I promise that you will see these people behind bars for life, or worse. In the mean time there will be others looking over you while I'm gone."

Ned spent the rest of the afternoon making travel arrangements. When he opened the envelope from Andropov he found some of the names and numbers which had been in Hovnaian's book. These however, were not encoded. It was clear that his work would be primarily in two cities – Moscow and Cairo. His knowledge of both languages and cultures would heighten his effectiveness.

He managed to secure the last seat aboard an Air France flight out of Newark's Liberty Airport at 7:30 that evening. It was in First Class, for which he was grateful. He had logged thousands of hours in the previous two decades with his 6'2" frame wedged in coach seats designed for ten year olds. He had flight companions of every type. There were business men who usually kept to themselves and often slept. Then there were the tourists who could not stop talking and were too excited to sleep.

Ned once sat next to John McEnroe, the tennis legend, who was on his way to do TV commentary at Wimbleton. On another flight from Copenhagen to Berlin, he sat by a French horn, seat-belted in place by his doting owner. And then there was the memorable trip from Miami to Santiago.

Ned's companion on that flight was a young mother who nursed her twin babies the entire trip. He spent a lot of time staring out the window.

This time he was going to travel in style. He took satisfaction in knowing that Andropov and his co-conspirators would somehow be picking up the tab.

Jill watched as Ned hastily packed one suitcase and a carry-on. From the closet he removed a long robe-like garment and began folding it neatly.

She laughed aloud. "Perhaps I've been a little hasty in assessing you. You're a little tall and muscular to be going in drag, aren't you?"

"Haven't you ever seen a *gallabaya*? It's a traditional robe worn by many Middle Eastern men. It's very practical. You can hike it when you work in the fields. It protects you from the hot sun. You don't even have to wear underwear."

"Don't tell me anymore. I get the idea."

Satisfied with his choice of clothing and toiletries, Ned retrieved his duffel bag. He sat on the bed and poured over a stack of passports and matching documents, selecting four sets to bring with him. He carefully loosened a false seam on the outer edge of the carry-on. It was secured with a very thin line of Velcro-like material. When he had safely stored three of the sets and closed the seam, Jill ran her fingers along the edge of the case.

"Wow. But why not pack them somewhere into the regular luggage?"

"If they look, they look inside. This hasn't failed me yet."

A horn sounded outside and Ned parted the curtains to see a Lincoln Town Car waiting out front. He moved his bags out into the hallway, turned to Jill and took her in his arms. Kissing her on the lips and then on the forehead, he said, "Wish me luck, kid. Better yet, pray for me."

She held him tightly. "I'm falling in love with you."

"That's what all the girls tell me."

She looked up into his eyes. "I'm serious."

"I know. We have to talk about the future."

He gave her one final squeeze and left her.

Just before five o'clock Ned called Kate Fowler to check in. "I thought I'd say goodbye, Kate. I'm going to take a little trip."

"Yes we know . You're on Air France flight 0019 to Paris, connecting to Moscow."

"Tsk, tsk, Agent Fowler. You've been spying on me."

"We're just doing our job. At least we can keep track of you until you leave the country. Take care of yourself, Richard. We'll keep an eye on Andropov and his crew."

"And, Jill?"

"Yes, you have my word. Between us and the N.Y.P.D. she will never be unguarded."

Rush hour traffic in Lower Manhattan again lived up to its reputation. The limo crawled cross-town, and pedestrians were passing them. The driver tried cutting through side streets, but so did many others. By the time they entered the Holland Tunnel it was nearly 5:45. If there was traffic on the New Jersey side, Ned feared he might miss his plane.

Thankfully at the exit of the tunnel everyone began accelerating. It was like popping the cork from a bottle. They sped down the Turnpike at seventy miles per hour. The toll booth and entrance to the airport were both congested so it was 6:30 by the time they pulled up to the International Terminal. He was relieved to see no line for the First Class check-in. The agent gave him a disapproving glance when she noted the time of his flight.

"You were supposed to be here an hour ago, *Monsieur*. We were just going to give your ticket to a stand-by passenger."

When he reached the gate, the plane was already half-loaded. He chided himself for his timing. It was not like Ned to be careless. He quickly used the men's room opposite the gate. As he washed his hands he stared at himself in the mirror.

Are you losing your edge Archangel?

Twenty minutes later the wheels of the massive Boeing 777 left the runway and they rose out over the Atlantic. The cabin lights were dimmed, and the last image in his mind before nodding off was that of the face of Jill gazing up at him.

CHAPTER THIRTY-THREE

Most travelers are exhausted by the time they negotiate flight transfers and time changes when going
to Eastern Europe or further east. Ned left the Moscow
terminal refreshed. He had developed an uncanny ability
to readjust his body clock when traveling to distant places.
He slept during planned intervals, and exercised in the area
between First Class and Coach, much to the amusement of
other passengers.

He was surprised at the ease with which he moved through
Russian customs. He had never seen agents so casual. The
tense atmosphere of Russian check-points, so long a part of
his experience, was gone.

The cold air outside slapped him in the face. He had not
left the terminal at Charles DeGaulle airport in Paris, except
to board the shuttle out to his connecting flight. Much like
New York, the "city of lights" had been enjoying a mild
autumn. Not so in Moscow, where winter had arrived early.
There was no snow, but the temperature hovered in the low
20's. Taxis and shuttle buses filled the pick-up area with
tailpipe vapors. Passengers waiting for their rides hunched
in heavy overcoats. It seemed that traditional Russian hats
appeared out of nowhere on every head.

Ned's mind wandered as he rode in the backseat of a
Lada taxicab. He had spent so much time in this city over

the years that it was almost like coming home. Faces flashed through his consciousness. People like the young KGB agent that Ned had turned who was now living in the U.S.A., or the beautiful art student he had befriended .... another Cheryl look-alike. And there were many nameless faces of those who had experienced T.R.U.T.H.'s form of justice at Ned's hand. They were all pawns in a political and ideological struggle. *Would that struggle ever end?*

He was brought back to the present by the humming of the driver, accompanying an old Russian standard on the radio. Ned playfully joined in, singing the words to the song. It was about love Russian-style.....love found, love misunderstood, love lost. The driver stared at Ned in the mirror with raised eye brows. *Another careless mistake!* He was violating one of the cardinal rules of "spook work": don't draw attention to yourself! There could be no room for failure on this mission. It wasn't just about him anymore. It was also about Jill, and Grace, and maybe about a new life and purpose.

Paying his fare, he made his way through the doors of the newly renovated Sputnik Hotel. There was no need to stay in a flea-bag hotel this trip. He was an American on a business trip hoping to convince Russian interests to champion the cause of capitalism in their country. Ned had stayed in all manner of accommodations and knew that even four-star hotels in Moscow could present challenges to one's sense of comfort and cleanliness. He was sure that the Sputnik would be more than adequate.

The desk clerk was cordial, and was fluent in English. After looking over Ned's passport and then running a copy of his American Express Card, he welcomed him warmly. "You should find everything in your room, Mr. Graham. If we can be of any further service to you at any time, just call the desk"

He then summoned the bell captain to bring Ned's belongings to his room.

By now Archangel had been either traveling or waiting to travel for almost twenty-four hours straight. He wasn't tired, but he figured a good meal and an evening's rest would keep him sharp. There was little that he could do until morning anyway. Before unpacking he made two calls on a throw-away cell phone, one of many he had brought with him. *Thank God for cell phones.* He thought that there was little chance that his calls could be monitored, but he was taking no risks. He bundled up and went out on his balcony, pulling the sliding door behind him.

The first call was answered right away. He said, "Hi, honey, this is Phil. I just wanted you to know I got here safely. I hope to be home in a few days. I miss you already."

Jill hesitated just a moment before she grasped his sense of caution. "I miss you too, baby. Hurry home." After a few more pleasantries, they ended the conversation.

Next Ned dialed the other number he had committed to memory. A female voice answered. It was Kate. "Global Enterprises, this is Penny speaking."

He thought of Kate actually being his secretary and smiled. "Penny, this is Philip. I thought I'd check in. I'm at the Sputnik. Anything going on?"

She didn't miss a beat. "Nothing new, boss. In your absence we're working our little tails off here though."

"I bet. Well, I'll give you a ring about this time each day to stay in touch. Please don't work too hard, Penny."

"I have to, boss. I don't want to jeopardize that Christmas bonus. Talk to you tomorrow."

• •

Archangel slept soundly that night….no dreams. He had not closed the darkening-drapes, so the morning light gradually brought him to consciousness. It was almost 8:00 o'clock. Before showering he dropped to the floor and did 50 push-ups and 100 sit-ups. Then as the warm water massaged his body, he engaged his mind in the plans for the day.

He knew he should have called Andropov the night before, but he couldn't force himself to do it. That would have to be the first order of business. Then a cup of coffee and a pastry in the shop in the lobby, and he would be ready to take on the bad guys waiting for him somewhere in Moscow.

At close to nine he put on his heavy coat, scarf and gloves and headed for the balcony. It felt much colder than the previous night. He dialed his nemesis in Brooklyn on another cell phone. It was now evening in New York. Someone else answered the phone and he had to wait for a time until he heard that familiar gravelly voice.

"Mr. Carlson, I was beginning to worry about you."

Ned was in no mood to apologize. "Well I'm here now Sergei. I will make contact today. You can trust me."

"No, I can't. That's why I've taken out some additional insurance on our venture. I have someone here who would like to say hello to you."

Ned was shaken. He felt an ache in the pit of his stomach. This could only mean one thing. The F.B.I. screwed up a simple task. He waited to hear Jill's voice. It was not to be.

"Uncle Ned?" That's all he heard or needed to hear. Andropov came back on the line.

"You have a beautiful young niece, Richard, or should I be calling you Ned. We will make her quite comfortable until our business is concluded. She will be unharmed."

He was speechless. "How…?"

"We were just lucky, Mr. Carlson. One of my associates spotted the two of you having lunch."

Anger was now replacing shock. "If anything happens to that girl, Andropov…"

"Save you breath, Richard. All will be well if you hold up your part of the bargain. In the meantime, I expect to hear from you every day. No more tardiness."

"You'll hear from me," Ned said flatly. And then he hung up. He felt nauseous.

Eating now was out of the question. Leaving the hotel Ned began walking. His mind was searching wildly. *Should I call Kate? No! I don't know where they're keeping her. I'll have to deal with this later. Gracie, don't let them know you're my daughter!*

Suddenly Ned stopped in the middle of the sidewalk. He heard singing. He looked up and found himself staring at a church sign – Trinity Church. He realized that he was in Sparrows Hill, an upscale neighborhood on the river, near Moscow State University. The church was massive, an historic structure which obviously predated Soviet Communism.

It wasn't a Sunday, but there was singing. It must have been some kind of Holy Day. Slipping in the massive front door, he found his way to a pew in the rear of the church. The hymn was over and the priest was just beginning his sermon. Ned's spirit was calmed as he took in the beauty of the sanctuary. He had visited many of the great cathedrals of the world, but the warmth that he felt in this place was much like that of the little mission church in San Marcos.

The priest spoke in a Russian dialect that drew both Ned's attention and concentration. He first read the words from Proverbs that had meant so much to Ned when was he was a child: *"Trust in the Lord with all your heart, and don't rely on your own insight. In all your ways acknowledge him, and he will make straight your paths."*

The homily seemed to be directed right to him. The priest must have used the word *труст*, trust, at least fifty times. And when Ned came forward to receive communion later in the service, as their eyes met, the priest smiled at him. When it ended, the priest went to the front door to shake hands with worshippers. Ned almost went out the side door, but decided to thank the holy man for his words. But when he took his hand, it was the priest who leaned to his ear, and in English said, "God will show you the way."

CHAPTER THIRTY-FOUR

Ned bounded down the steps of the church. He retraced his way back to the hotel, picked up a coffee and took it to his room. Grabbing the chenille bedspread off the bed, he wrapped himself in it and made his way to the balcony again. He dialed the local number that Andropov had given him.

It was a strong, but definitely feminine voice that answered. He had been instructed to say only, "the transaction is ready to be made." He did so in his best Russian.

The woman responded, "You don't even have an accent, my friend. With your predecessor I had to speak only English." She hesitated only a moment. "Where are you staying?"

When hearing it was the Sputnik she said, "There are benches outside the Administration Building of the University. It is only a short walk from your hotel. Bring a newspaper and be reading it on the last bench on the right side, at 4 o'clock." Then he only heard a dial tone.

By mid-afternoon it had dropped below freezing, but there was little wind. As Archangel settled on the assigned bench, the light was beginning to fade in the eastern sky. There were people moving from place to place on campus, but he was the only one who was sitting on a bench. Still he opened the newspaper which he had purchased at the hotel.

She seemed to appear out of nowhere. He recognized the voice and looked up from the paper. She was strikingly beautiful. A woman in her 40's, she was close to six feet tall, with an athletic build. From beneath her knitted cap, amid wisps of blonde hair, peered the greenest eyes he had ever seen.

"Please stand up and greet me," she said. He stood up and she threw her arms around him and kissed him on both cheeks. He responded to her embrace. "Walk with me," she ordered.

Ned found the situation humorous. "I just love Russian hospitality…and I don't even know your name."

His contact was not smiling. "We must be careful. You may call me Tatiana. Our business will be brief. First, tell me what happened to Hovnanian."

He measured his words, not wanting to destabilize the situation. "Let's just say he was a greedy man, and his partners thought it would be in everyone's best interest to utilize someone else, namely *me.*"

"And you are…?"

"My name is Philip Graham, and I can assure you that all is in place to conclude this arrangement. You have the merchandise, we have the needed capital, and I will facilitate the transfer. It can be done in a matter of days."

"OK, Mr. Graham, tell me how."

Ned cleared his throat. "This is not complicated. When I have transferred the funds, I will meet you again, authenticate the material, and then wait with you until the money has entered your account. Then I will be on my way. I have written instructions here as to how I want the goods wrapped and packed. It is my understanding that it will fit into an average suitcase."

"That's correct. But how will you get it out of Russia?"

"That's not your concern. Do you have the account numbers in Zurich where you want the funds to go?"

"I have them with me."

She handed him an envelope from her purse. He removed another from his jacket and handed it to her. They had been walking slowly the entire time, working their way down toward the river. He finally turned to her.

"This will go smoothly, Tatiana. I must leave Moscow for a couple of days, but will call you as soon as I return. We can make the exchange at that time."

She nodded, but before she could reply Ned reached for her, embraced her, kissed her, and whispered, "Farewell, my love, until we meet again."

Heading back in the direction of the Sputnik Ned could sense that he was not alone. He knew that he and Tatiana were never far from prying eyes, and that he would be watched until he left Moscow. The game clock was now running. There was no turning back.

Passing a restaurant within sight of the hotel, Ned realized that the cause of the headache he was experiencing was probably hunger. He had nothing to eat or drink since coffee that morning. Turning back, he entered the eatery. The place was full of young people, some with laptops propped up in front of them.

He was seated near the front window within full view of the boulevard. The condensation on the glass exaggerated the lights of passing cars. The waiter dropped a menu in front of him without saying a word, and moved off to another table where he obviously knew an attractive young woman. Glancing at the restaurant's name at the top of the menu. Ned laughed aloud. He looked around and everyone seemed to be looking at him. He playfully shrugged, and reread the name of the establishment where he had chosen to eat. Loosely translated it was called, "The Place to Ponder."

The food was excellent despite the service. Ned had regained his appetite and did little pondering during the meal. Russian food was not his favorite, but it was always hardy and nourishing. When he paid the bill his stomach was full and his headache gone. The tip he left his waiter reflected the service.

Back on the street he noticed a man seemingly walking in the opposite direction. It was the same person who had passed him and Tatiana as they strolled the campus. *O the games we play.*

He took out a cell phone and dialed Kate's number. He was interrupted by the message, "all circuits are busy." He tried twice more and got the same message. He decided the call could wait, and immediately phoned Andropov, who answered the call himself.

"Very good, Richard. You've called twice within a day."

Ned felt nothing but distaste for this man. "Put Grace on the phone," he demanded.

"She's here, but I can't always guarantee she'll be accessible to the phone."

He heard Grace being summoned to the phone. "Hi, Uncle Ned."

"Are you doing OK Gracie? I am so sorry that you got caught up in this."

"They're treating me pretty good. I know you'll work this out, whatever it is."

Good girl. Her voice was strong.

Andropov interrupted them. "That's enough, Richard. I told you that she would be all right."

Annoyed, but satisfied for the moment, Ned put his mind to business. "Everything is set on this end. I am heading to Cairo tomorrow. I don't expect it to be as smooth there. I still don't understand their willingness to turn over all this money to you before receiving the material."

"We have done business with them before. This is how it is done. They know that they'll get what they are paying for. This is pocket change for them, Richard. It just keeps flowing out of the ground thick and black, and turns immediately into money."

Ned couldn't stand listening to Andropov even a moment longer. "You'll be hearing from me."

****

The next morning he settled into an aisle seat aboard an Aeroflot jet heading for the Middle East. He never felt very secure on the Russian airline, recalling horror stories he had heard from many. If he could have found an available seat on another carrier on such short notice, he would have gladly done so.

After a bumpy take-off, he stretched out and reflected on his conversation with Andropov, and what he might expect in Egypt. He wondered how the Russian and his cronies had maneuvered themselves into such an advantageous position as middlemen in illicit arm sales. They had everything to gain and nothing to lose. He could see how their use of Hovnanian, and now of himself, insulated them from any personal risk. He almost admired them for their resourcefulness.

Ned was alone in his row of seats. He saw it as a commentary on his life. He had grown accustomed to it, but on this day he was more than alone – he was lonely. Since Jill appeared he knew that he no longer wanted to be by himself. He wished that she was sitting next to him, that they could be talking about mundane things, even laughing and flirting with one another like normal couples who cared about one another. *Do I dare use the word love?*

CHAPTER THIRTY-FIVE

Grace Dickson had now been missing for more than forty-eight hours since she was snatched off the sidewalk into a waiting bakery truck. Despite her situation she felt reasonably calm. Hearing her father's voice gave her added courage. Up to this point she had been treated fairly well. She was a fan of the TV show, "Without a Trace." The thought crossed her mind that a new script was being written here for some future episode.

When Andropov hung up the phone he stared at her for a moment. She returned his gaze.

"You are a strong young woman, Miss Dickson. You share some traits with your uncle."

My father! I am my father's daughter. "I'll take that as a compliment. Now let me be alone."

"As you wish."

He nodded to a sleazy looking young man who had been Grace's keeper since she arrived. He led her, hands bound, to a back room and cut her plastic ties. He watched as she sat down on the lumpy twin bed. He had been undressing her with his eyes since the moment she came. She hoped that he would never get the chance to act out his fantasies.

When he left, she shivered involuntarily and looked around once again at her surroundings. The room was furnished in what might be described as "Early Salvation

Army." A chrome-trimmed dinette table sat in one corner, and was complimented by two folding chairs. Empty take-out boxes and bags were strewn on the floor nearby. A gaudy blue dresser stood against one wall, and a mahogany end table, missing pieces of its veneer, sat near the bed. The room had only one light, a low wattage bulb screwed into a ceiling fixture.

Ever since that day in the restaurant, Grace had been turning over the circumstances of her life in her mind. Her resentment for her father was momentary. When she replayed his words to her that day, she realized what a sacrifice it had been for him to entrust her to her aunt and uncle. *No, mom and dad! They will always be my mom and dad.*

Now she understood the extraordinary bond that Ned Reed had shared with her family and especially with her over the years. Certain events and conversations now could be seen for what they really were – the pining of a father for the daughter he could never claim as his own.

"Well, not anymore," she said aloud.

She jumped as the door opened and "Casanova" entered with a bag from Burger King. She sat at the table as he placed it there, and then waited for him to leave. Instead, he pulled up the other chair and studied her. It was getting harder and harder to tolerate his presence.

"You may leave now. I prefer to eat alone."

He continued to ogle her. "I am not a bad guy, Grace. You have been alone so much. I could come and keep you company tonight. I am told that I'm a good lover."

She lost it. "Never!" She reached across the table to hit him. He grabbed her wrist and twisted it. She screamed.

There was a noise behind them. Sergei Andropov appeared in the doorway. To his young colleague he simply said, "Out!" Then he came and sat in the seat that had just been vacated.

"Miss Dickson, I would suggest you not toy with my little brother. I will not be responsible for what he does if you continue to tease him."

Grace continued to rub her wrist. "It wasn't me. Keep him away from me."

He did not reply. He turned and left the room, slamming the door behind him.

CHAPTER THIRTY-SIX

Next to New York, Cairo was Ned's favorite city in the world. The plane's approach afforded him a view of the city itself to the southwest, and on this unusually clear day, a glimpse in the distance of the three pyramids in Giza.

He had decided to retain his current identity. After some brief hassling by Egyptian custom police, he was allowed to proceed out into the terminal. He had made no prior arrangements for accommodations, but was well aware of his options. Besides, he hoped that he could conclude his business quickly.

He stood in the baggage area and called the next number on his list. A monotone Arabic voice came on the line. *"Aiwa."*

"My name is Philip Graham, and I am here to arrange for delivery of your ordered merchandise."

The man responded in broken English. "Where are you now, Mr. Graham?"

"At Cairo Airport."

"Be in the pick-up area in half an hour."

The line went dead. It struck Ned that in his line of work people rarely said good-bye to one another. He put his belongings in a rental locker and made his way to the ground transportation exit. Several flights must have arrived simultaneously because the area was crowded with travelers vying for taxis and vans. He found a place close to the curb and waited.

In just a few minutes a Mercedes Sedan pulled up in front of him. A young man in an Ohio State sweatshirt left the driver's seat and came around to him.

"Mr. Graham?" he said. At least that's what he tried to say.

"Aiwa," Ned replied.

The man smiled and opened the rear door.

"Schuckran" (Thank you), said Ned.

Another smile. *"Afwan."*.

Before they left the airport exit, Ned and his new friend, Mohammed, were into a lively conversation in Arabic. The man had a brother living in Cincinnati. He hoped to visit there one day. Ned finally got around to asking him where they were going.

The light atmosphere quickly changed. Ned's question reminded the young man that he was on a mission. His response was terse. "You will know when we get there." Then he set his face toward the windshield and never spoke another word.

As they proceeded down the broad tree-lined boulevard toward the city, Ned absorbed the sights and sounds of this vibrant city. Stately buildings, most of them governmental, passed before his eyes. But this was a place of sharp contrasts. He knew that two or three blocks to either side were probably dilapidated dwellings, or even small plots of land being worked by destitute families.

Men in business suits mingled with farmers dressed in coarse *gallabayas*. Women, most of whom wore some form of head covering, paraded by in designer jeans and high-heeled shoes. Occasionally a smartly dressed man would pass, accompanied by his wife, clad in a full black *berka*. Only her eyes could be seen.

Traffic slowed to a crawl as cars, trucks, mini-cabs, donkey carts, and ancient motor cycles competed for the slightest advantage. Lanes were nonexistent, and pedestrians were forced to cross streets between and around vehicles.

It seemed like Cairo was bursting at the seams. At twenty-two million, it had been growing by a million a year as people descended on it from the countryside. Vast brick tenements were being constructed everywhere.

Ned's driver took a left turn and headed south rather than into the heart of the city. In the distance he could see the Citadel high above the city. It was a fortress built around one of the largest mosques in the Muslim world. It had been named for one of Egypt's great rulers, Mohammed Ali. To his surprise the Mercedes went straight to the Citadel. In the drop-off area, Mohammed found his voice again.

"Go into the mosque. I will be waiting here when you are finished."

Ned had visited this shrine many times. It was massive. Removing his shoes he tucked them under his arm. Persian rugs covered the entire floor of the mosque. The ornate ceiling loomed eight stories above him. Hundreds of tourists in all manner of dress were snapping pictures from every possible angle. Several women wore green robe-like garments provided them to cover tank-tops and shorts.

He waited, watching people come and go. Finally a bearded man in a *gallabaya* approached him. "Welcome to Egypt, Mr.Graham. Please follow me."

They walked out on to a broad terrace which overlooked the vast city of Cairo. His host turned to him. "I understand your Arabic is quite good – much better than my English. Do you mind?"

"I would prefer it," replied Ned.

"Do you wonder why I brought you here?" Extending his hand toward the view he asked, "What do you see, Mr. Graham? Look at the landscape. What do you see?"

Ned understood immediately. In every direction the city was dotted with stately minarets, rising from hundreds of mosques. He decided to play dumb. "Perhaps you should tell me."

"It is the future of the world. Allah wills it! Perhaps not in our lifetime, but Islam will prevail."

Ned had heard enough. He wanted to take this man, who in the name of his religion would annihilate innocent human beings, and hurl him from the parapet. Instead, he coolly replied.

"Thank you for your lesson, but I think it's time we discussed our business. Are you the person I am to talk to, or will you take me to someone else?"

The man smiled. "I like you. Unlike the other one they sent, you speak my language, and you don't try to flatter me. I am the man. Let's talk about our transaction."

CHAPTER THIRTY-SEVEN

The two negotiators slipped into the rear seat of the Mercedes. Mohammed had parked it in the center of the parking lot. As if on cue he left the driver's seat and locked the doors with his key-ring remote. Ned and the other man, who would not give his name, watched through tinted glass as he wandered over to a refreshment kiosk.

The bearded one turned to Ned. "OK, my friend. What news do you bring me?"

"The news is that your goods are ready for delivery. I am here to arrange for your payment, and then will go and bring them back to you. The price as agreed is twenty million American dollars. It is to be sent to an account in the Cayman Islands for which I will give you the routing numbers."

The man shook his head from side to side. "What is this twenty million? I am prepared to pay you fifteen, and not a *piaster* more."

Ned was ready for this. "I am familiar with the bargaining ways of your culture. That's why I'm insulted that you would attempt to renegotiate an already agreed upon price. I see no reason for us to continue this conversation."

He grabbed the door handle and began opening it. His host took his arm. "Hold on there. This is the first time we have met, Mr. Graham. We have never discussed money before."

Ned re-closed the door. "When you dealt with Hovnanian you dealt with me. We can either conclude it now, or I will take our business elsewhere."

The man smiled as if this encounter had never happened. "I told you that I like you. You will get your twenty million."

Ned handed him an envelope from his pocket which contained the numbers for Andropov's off-shore accounts. In passing it over he said, "Now that we have this out of the way, may I ask you a question?"

"You may ask."

"What was your arrangement with Mr. Hovnanian?"

With an insincere look of surprise, he replied, "I don't know what you mean?"

"I know that he was working both ends of this deal to his benefit. I have no such plans. I'm just curious – it's just between you and me."

Another smile. "I suppose it doesn't matter now. The original price was to be twenty-two million. For just half a million your predecessor offered to convince the other side that twenty was all that they could get. A clever plan, yes?"

"Where he is he's not going to get to spend any of it."

"Such is fate, Mr. Graham. But we have saved even more money, haven't we?"

The man leaned over the front seat and sounded the horn. Mohammed tossed his coffee cup into a can and came immediately. The two Arabs repeated their seat-switching maneuver and the mysterious stranger disappeared to the rear of the car.

The ride back to the airport was far worse than coming. Every intersection seemed to be in gridlock. Policemen in white uniforms tried in vain to move traffic along, often jawing with drivers who were ignoring their directions. Mohammed was once again his amiable self, and spoke in run-on sentences about everything imaginable. Ned did not encourage him, and soon stopped listening as he retreated into his own thoughts.

He should have been pleased at the ease with which his assignment was progressing. Despite his avarice, Hovnanian had successfully laid the groundwork for the deal. A part of Ned felt disappointment that his role turned out to be little more than a delivery boy. Yet experience told him that things were rarely simple, and that the whole deal could unravel at any time.

He was tempted to retrieve his baggage from the locker and try to find space on the next flight out of Egypt. Instinct reminded him that his arrival and departure on the same day might raise a red flag with authorities. He could probably talk his way through it, but this was not the time to be careless. Instead, he proceeded to the transportation area again and found a seat in a quiet corner. He pulled out his personal phone, switched it on, and noticed that he had two missed calls – both had left messages.

The first was from Jill. He had given her this number in case of a dire emergency. Immediately he dialed the apartment in New York. She answered breathlessly, and when she heard his voice she broke down into muffled sobs.

"Jill, are you all right? What's happened?"

She regained a measure of composure. "O Ned, I had to hear your voice. I don't want you doing this. Just come home. I don't want to lose you."

He felt agitation and pity at the same moment. "Well you almost lost me to heart failure. Jill, you've got to hold it together for me. Everything has gone just as planned. It will be over in a few days."

"But…"

"Stop! Listen to me. It's going to be OK – I promise. But I've got to concentrate on what I'm doing, not worrying about you. Please, hang in there. We're going to make it."

Her voice was almost normal now. "I'm sorry. I love you."

"I, I love you too. Now go find an old movie on the tube and chill out. I'll talk to you soon."

When he hung up he breathed a sigh of relief. Jill had a torturous job in this – waiting. He had no doubt that he himself would be a bit stir-crazy by now, if all he could do was wait as others were determining his future.

The second call was from Andropov. Ned thought that this was a good sign. It might signify a slight change in the balance of power between them. To his astonishment the return call was answered by Grace.

"Uncle Ned?"

"How are you honey?"

"So far so good."

That's all she was permitted to say. The Russian came on the line. "You see, Richard – or Ned. Everything is just fine here. Now tell me about your work in Cairo."

Ned felt the subtle shift in their relationship. He was running the show now. He needed to press the advantage. "It was touch and go here, Sergei. They tried to cut the price dramatically."

"You didn't give in?"

"No, but the deal nearly caved in on us. In the end we will get what we asked for."

"Good man."

"Begin checking your accounts, Andropov. The transfer could happen at any time. Get a pen and paper ready. I want to give you the numbers for Zurich."

Following the recitation of numbers, Ned concluded the conversation quickly without giving the Russian the opportunity to respond. "I'm going back to Moscow, and will then bring the goods to Egypt. It's too risky to fly commercial, so it may take a bit longer to complete this. You will hear from me."

Ned got his luggage and summoned a cab. He bargained with the driver for a price of thirty Egyptian pounds to take him back to the city. En-route he switched passports. At the reception desk at the Ramses Hilton, a pretty clerk named Mary smiled broadly when she saw him.

"Mr. Davis, we haven't seen you in a long time. Do you have a reservation with us?"

"I'm afraid my stay was unexpected."

"Never a problem for you, sir."

CHAPTER THIRTY-EIGHT

The sound of Ned's voice gave Jill Hovnanian renewed hope. After their brief conversation, she settled into a recliner in the living room and began browsing through an old photo album. She had found it on the top shelf of one of Ned's many bookcases. The early pages contained snapshots of his family of origin. His parents were handsome people. He looked a great deal like his father. It was that smile and those expressive eyes.

There were three children in the Reed family, and it was clear that Ned was the youngest sibling by many years. In one family portrait his father wore a clerical collar. *He didn't tell me that his dad was a preacher, but I shouldn't be surprised. He's such a spiritual person.*

Not far into the album John Henry Reed disappeared. *What happened to him?* After that there was an occasional picture of Ned and his mother, amid a series of maturing school photos. His interest in sports was underscored by various poses in baseball, basketball and soccer uniforms. Most of the pictures taken apparently during high school days included a strikingly beautiful blonde.

Several pages were then blank. When Ned's pictorial life history continued it was another young woman who filled the pages. *Cheryl.* One photo after another showed a young couple who were very much in love. On its own page was an 8 X 10 portrait of them on their wedding day.

Jill suddenly felt great sadness. She too was happy on the day of her marriage to David Hovnanian. They had met on a blind date in Georgetown, and saw one another almost daily for several months. He was good looking and self-confident. He showered her with gifts and affection. As a boyfriend he was charming. But almost from the beginning David, the husband, was a different man. In public he was still entertaining, but at home he was moody and undemon-strative. He started traveling extensively with his work. Jill figured that they had been together only half of the four years they had been married. *What happened to you David? What happened to us?*

She scanned the remaining pages of the album. It was Ned and Cheryl on their bikes, Ned and Cheryl washing a red sports car, Ned and Cheryl camping on the top of a mountain – and they were always smiling. Then suddenly the pictures ended. On the final page was a single close-up of a new-born baby, fully wrapped in pink. *And you must be the other woman.*

And that was it. It was as if Ned's life had ended that day. As if there was nothing more worthy of note, nothing further to smile about, nothing to celebrate. Jill's eyes filled with tears. *I want to help you smile again, Ned Reed.*

She set the album aside and her eyes were drawn to the ornate cross Ned had prominently hung over the fireplace. She gazed at it for several minutes.

> *God, I guess you know a thing or two about human sadness and suffering. You DO understand, don't you? I want to know you the way Ned does!*
> *Protect him Lord. Bring him home.*
> *And....I want to trust you with my future, with or without this wonderful man.*

As if propelled by an unknown force, Jill rose and went immediately to the kitchen. She took the phone from its cradle and dialed the number of a farm in the hills of Western Maryland. A woman answered the call.

"Mom?"

"Jill! Is it you?"

"Yes mom. I hope it's not too early to call?"

"Oh honey, I don't care what time it is. Are you all right? Has something happened?

"Yes, a lot has happened. But first I want to tell you that I love you, and that I'm so sorry for cutting you and dad out of my life. Can you ever forgive me?"

"Jill, we have never stopped loving you, and we have been waiting for this call. Come home."

So this is how the "Prodigal" must have felt. The two of them cried softly together. Then Jill took an audible breath. "Mom, can you get dad on the other line?"

After James Brooke and his daughter shared some emotional words, she told them about David's death. She assured them that she was safe, and that the murder was almost solved. They urged her to come home. She promised to do so, but first had to arrange for her husband's burial. She didn't tell them about Ned. *I don't know what to say about him at this moment.*

She hung up the phone and found herself flooded with her own pictorial memories of childhood. There was a happy girl feeding the hogs before school, jumping from the hay loft hand-in-hand with her little sister on warm summer afternoons. There were the trips to town in the back of the pick-up on Saturday mornings, highlighted by visits to Clausen's candy store. There were the country dances at the Akins' barn.

It was all such an embarrassment to her when she arrived on the campus of the University of Maryland. *Silly girl! That's when YOU stopped smiling.*

The rest was a blur. The boring job at the Department of Labor, endless parties with Washington's nightclub crowd, and finally paradise, found and lost so quickly with David Hovnanian.

O God, I want to smile again – from the inside.

CHAPTER THIRTY-NINE

Archangel enjoyed a leisurely meal in the restaurant atop the Ramses. Below him flowed the mighty Nile. Tourist boats made their way up and down the river amid ancient *feluccas*. A million vehicles continued to clog the streets and bridges of Cairo. Headlights blinked on and off in the evening darkness. Ned couldn't understand why they just didn't leave them on all the time.

Far above the chaos of the city the only sounds to reach Ned's ears were the clinking of plates and silverware as waiters efficiently plied their trade, and the subdued chords of old standards being played by a young man on a grand piano in the middle of the room.

In his mind he replayed the awkward phone conversation with Jill. There was so much hanging in the balance for her and for them in this drama. The pianist slid into a rendition of "New York, New York" and he realized how much he wished she were sitting across the table from him now. It could be any city, any restaurant. He just wanted this to be over and for them to be together. He looked out again at all the lights reflecting on the Nile. "Perhaps," he thought, "I'll bring her back someday to this wonderful city."

Well-fed now and looking forward to a restful evening, Ned entered the elevator and punched the button for the nineteenth floor. Just as the door was about to close, a hand reached in and it parted to reveal an impeccably dressed Middle Eastern man. His suit and shoes were definitely European, his tie of the finest silk. Ned had seen him sitting alone on the other side of the dining room.

As the door closed again, the man turned to him and said to him in Arabic, "May I ask you to join me in the lobby for a brief time, Mr. Graham?" He pressed the L on the panel. Curiosity caused Ned to let the door open and close at his floor. Once in the lobby the man guided him to a table in the back of a lounge.

When they were seated, Ned took the initiative. "To what do I owe this honor, Mr......?"

"Wahed. My name is Sameer Wahed."

"You're number one, Sameer."

"I beg your pardon?"

"Number one in Arabic - *wahed.*"

The man faintly smiled. "Yes, of course. I won't keep you long, Mr.Graham. I have a proposition for you sir. You have been in business dealings with some of my associates here in Cairo, yes?"

"If you say so, Mr. Wahed. What can I do for you?"

"As you know, we are involved in the import/export trade of rare and expensive items. We are looking for someone with your apparent skills to represent our interests outside the Middle East."

Ned wanted to end the conversation at this moment. Instead he replied, "Mr. Wahed, it seems from what I've seen that you are mostly exporters of money. It's the imported items that really interest me. Besides, why would you think I'd have any interest in supporting your cause?"

"Money, Mr. Graham. More money than you can dream of. That should be cause enough."

He had heard enough. "I'll tell you what, Sameer. Let me complete my current assignment and then we can speak further about this."

"So you would consider our proposition?"

"For more money than I can imagine – of course. But let's not get ahead of ourselves. Do you have a number where I can reach you when I return to Cairo?"

The man handed him a business card which gave his name, phone number, and a corporate name, "Imagination Traders, Ltd." It was written in English and Arabic. Ned placed the card in his shirt pocket and pushed back from the table.

"If you would excuse me, Mr. Wahed, it's been a long day."

Back in his room, he moved immediately to the balcony. It was a relatively mild night, in stark contrast to the frigid air of Moscow. He now had only a few throw-away phones left. He dialed Kate Fowler in New York, who answered in her secretarial persona.

"I'm going to have to start calling you Penny all the time, Kate. Anyway, the coast is clear so we can talk freely."

"OK, boss. It's good to hear your voice. What's up?"

"We're getting close. Now the two of us have to talk coordination because everyone has to move when I say 'go.' Has the State Department done its work?"

"Yes, the *federales* in Russia and Egypt are as anxious to nail these guys as we are. We have their complete cooperation."

"OK. As of tonight I have some additional work for them. The Egyptians have to be ready to move on another part of their operation." He gave her Wahed's information. "Any more activity at the Russian Club in Brooklyn, Kate?"

"It's been very quiet – almost too quiet."

"I have to tell you something, and you have to promise me that you won't act on it until I'm there. So promise me!"

"What are you talking about?"

"Just promise!"

"OK, OK, I promise."

Ned sighed. "Andropov is holding my daughter, who he thinks is my niece."

"Jesus, Joseph, and Mary!"

"Her name is Grace Dickson."

"O man. Her disappearance has been front page in The Daily News. We can't just sit on this thing."

"You can and you will. I don't know for sure where she's being kept. I just know that she is all right at this point. I've talked to her, Kate. I won't risk her life. I'm going to hold you to your promise, even if you have to withhold it from your superiors."

"You've got my word."

"My sister and her husband must be worried sick. I want you to call Kara and Garrett. Tell them that Gracie is OK. Tell them that this is not a ransom situation. Tell them that she will be free in a few days. Tell them not to breathe a word of this to anyone. And tell them that Ned will bring her home."

"Why don't you call them?"

"I just can't, Kate. I don't know if I can handle it. I don't want them anymore distressed than they are already."

With genuine sadness in her tone, Kate replied, "I'll call them as soon as we hang up. How are you going to do this, Richard? I don't even know what to call you now."

"Call me Ned. I need you to do one more thing. I will need a plane waiting for me on the runway in Cairo the moment this hits the fan. I want to be in Brooklyn within hours. Do you understand?"

"I understand, but I don't see how I can pull those kind of strings, Ned."

"Just do it! I don't care if you have to skyjack Air Force One. Check with my superiors, Kate. They have the clout to make it happen."

"Ned, I hope you know what you're doing."

"I hope so too. I'm returning to Moscow tomorrow. I can't risk flying on any airline with this stuff, so it will take a couple of days to get back here."

"Why don't we get the Russians and the Egyptians to give you a free pass, Ned?"

"I don't trust the Russians to even let this material out of the country, and I don't trust the Egyptians to let it in. I have to do it my way."

"And do you want the President himself waiting for you in Air Force One?"

"I'm not laughing, Kate. This has got to happen. If I lose Grace, I don't care what happens to the rest of this. If this can't be arranged, I'm pulling out. Is that clear?"

"Very clear."

Ned gave Kate Kara's phone number in New Jersey and told her that he would call again within twenty-four hours to finalize plans.

It was still a mild night in Cairo, but as Ned stared out at the Nile, he was gripped by a chill more intense than anything he had felt in Moscow.

O Lord, get us all through this!

CHAPTER FORTY

He was certain now that he was being followed wherever he went. They were good but not *that* good. He gazed out the window of the taxi on his way to the airport. He chuckled at the thought of anyone attempting to follow his cab in the vehicular madness around him.

The night before he had booked a flight that would eventually get him to Moscow by late afternoon. After viewing his documents airport security led him to a windowless room where he waited alone for thirty minutes. *What now?* He began to wonder if the Egyptian government was getting cold feet.

He was aroused by a heated exchange taking place right outside the door. He only caught some of the conversation. Apparently an officer was chastising a subordinate. When the door opened the officer appeared and was smiling as he approached Ned.

"Mr. Graham, we are so sorry for the delay. There was a misunderstanding here. My men should not have detained you. We have a cart waiting to take you directly to the plane."

Five minutes later he was ascending the steps to board his flight. All the seats were taken but his own. As he moved down the aisle he overheard conversations in many different languages – most of which he could understand. *What would Egypt do without its tourists?*

It was a smooth flight and his transfer to the Moscow leg in Paris was uneventful. He settled into deep thought. With each contact things were becoming more complex. There were many parties involved now, and each had to follow through, trusting their equally suspicious co-conspirators. He felt like a circus performer trying to juggle several fiery objects. There would be no mercy if one was dropped. And the punishment would fall on Grace.

Safely through Russian customs, he made two more calls. Andropov was showing the strain. "Where are you, Richard?"

"Moscow airport. Let me speak to Grace."

The Russian was clearly annoyed. "You can speak with her all you want in a couple of days."

"I want to hear her voice!"

This time all he was permitted to hear was Gracie calling out from somewhere across the room. Andropov was pushing back. "OK, Richard, now just listen to me. We've received payment from our friends in the Middle East. We are prepared to make the transfer to Moscow as soon as you tell us that you have the goods."

Ned sighed to himself. "That call should come within the next day."

It was Andropov's turn to hang up. Ned was left in silence. Next he phoned Kate Fowler. "This is it, Kate," he said as soon as he heard her voice. "The next call will set everything in motion."

She was ready for this call. "All is in place in Moscow, Ned. All the principals have now been identified and will be apprehended the moment the exchange is made. Then you are on your own. Get out of there fast. We can't be absolutely sure that the Russians will let this go any further."

"I need you to arrange one last piece, Kate. It's my ticket back to Cairo." He then explained in detail what had to be done.

"OK, O wise one. It will be done for you."

"And what about my plane in Cairo?"

"I couldn't get Air Force One. Would you settle for a Navy jet?"

"Thanks, Kate. Any other news?"

"The whole city is still buzzing about Grace's disappearance. All remains quiet with Andropov and his merry band."

"I'm going to hang up and make *the* call now. Wish me luck. Better yet, do some praying."

• •

Ned noted a slight tremor as he touched the number pad on his phone. He had been running on adrenaline for days now. This was not the time to falter. Tatiana was obviously waiting for his call. She answered, "Good evening, Mr. Graham."

"I'm back," he said.

"I know. Someone is watching you right now. When we end this conversation he will take you back to the Sputnik. A room has been reserved in your name. At eight this evening you are to call room service and order a light meal."

"All right. What then?"

"Just order the meal."

• •

On the ride from the airport Ned tried to engage his driver in conversation. The man would not respond. The desk person at the hotel was the same one as before. It was almost 7:30 pm by the time he closed his door. He needed a shower and a shave.

At precisely eight o'clock he ordered some soup and a sandwich from room service. Within twenty minutes there was a knock at the door. Slowly he opened it to a waiting service cart being pushed by the same man who had driven him from the airport. He was wearing the distinctive uniform of the hotel staff, a maroon suit with a monogrammed space-craft on the breast pocket.

The Russian wheeled the cart into the room and before Ned could close the door, Tatiana slipped in behind him. "Thank you, Annatoly. Now leave us alone."

Ned had still not heard the man speak. As instructed he left the room and pulled the door closed behind him. Archangel was feeling uncharacteristically nervous. *This is not the time for second thoughts.* Forcing a smile, he quipped, "You look lovely tonight, my love."

She returned a forced smile. "Ah, Mr. Graham, we mustn't mix business with pleasure. We both have our jobs to do. Let's get on with it, shall we?"

She removed the cloth which had completely covered the cart. On top was the food that he had ordered. The room had already begun filling with the aroma of potato soup. On a second shelf there was what appeared to be an over-sized attaché case. Next to it was a plain cardboard box. On the lowest shelf, just inches above the floor, was a stack of colorful garments.

Tatiana went right to work. She tossed Ned a light-weight garment which resembled a space-suit. He recognized it as hazmat protective wear. Without a word they both put on the suits, along with matching booties, headgear and gloves.

"This is only a precaution," she finally said. "Neither of us should be at any risk."

Reaching into the box she brought out a small handheld device. "Mr. Graham, this will alert us to low levels of radia-tion. Please place the case on the bed."

Ned carefully lifted it from the cart. The small case must have weighed fifty pounds. The woman turned on the device and scanned it over and around the case. There was no response.

"As you can see, it is completely safe. This case is lined in lead. Now I'm going to open it briefly. Look quickly, Mr. Graham, and then observe my little friend here. She tapped the handheld instrument."

She aligned the code numbers on the two latches and opened the case. He took note of the contents. Embedded in thick insulation were three stainless steel canisters. Tatiana waved the meter across the interior and it immediately began emitting a low-pitched crackling sound. Ned noticed the needle rise slowly into the green zone of a gauge. She quickly closed the case and turned off the device.

"We are perfectly safe. I can assure you that nothing has been contaminated in this room. You may disrobe now."

The gear was stowed again on the cart, and Tatiana turned to Ned. "Now, it's your turn."

Without hesitation he retrieved another phone from the night stand and made the call. Andropov answered. "We are ready, Richard. The money will be transferred within minutes. Call me from your final stop."

"OK," was all Ned said in response, and then terminated the call. They both seemed to catch a deep breath at the same time. He then gestured toward the cart. "Will you join me for a bite to eat while we wait?"

She shook her head. "I have no appetite, and I plan to leave very soon."

Actually Ned was very hungry. He sat in an arm chair with a tray in his lap and devoured the meal. Just as he was dabbing his chin for the last time the room's phone rang. It startled both of them. He answered and then handed the receiver to Tatiana. She said nothing but when she hung up she smiled at Ned.

"Our business is concluded, Mr. Graham." On her way to the door she kissed him on the cheek. "Perhaps it would have been fun at a different time and place...."

As she exited, her silent partner came into the room and removed the cart. In a moment they were both gone.

CHAPTER FORTY-ONE

Ned drove through the night.

After notifying Kate Fowler to unleash Russian authorities to arrest the conspirators in Moscow, he had hastily packed his things. He took the elevator to the ground floor, exited a rear door and emerged into a small parking lot behind the hotel. It was completely deserted. He selected a late model BMW and within minutes had the door open and the engine running – he hadn't lost his touch. Returning to the room, he gathered his belongings and carried them all in one hand while lugging the heavy case in the other. After stowing everything in the trunk, he got behind the wheel, adjusted the mirrors, and slowly pulled out on to a side street.

It was now several hours later. He had actually welcomed the drive because it gave him time to think about the future – about Grace, and about Jill. He had to stop for fuel once in a small town along the route. It turned out to be the only station open during the entire trip. Taking a side road near the border, his crossing into the Ukraine was uneventful. At a little before five in the morning he came over a rise, and the lights of Odessa came into view. Beyond it was total darkness – the Black Sea.

Instead of entering the city itself, Ned turned on a side road heading west. Just as the sun appeared on the horizon in his rear-view mirror, he came upon a deserted military airstrip in the middle of nowhere. At the far end of the overgrown runway sat a sleek aircraft. A lone figure sat on the ground leaning against one of its tires.

Ned pulled the BMW to within fifty feet of the plane, turned off the engine and waited. The man eyed him briefly and then made his way over to the car. Ned lowered the window.

"Are you looking for a ride, sir?" The accent was definitely American, from somewhere below the Mason-Dixon Line.

"Yes," said Ned. "Where might you be heading?"

"How about Egypt, sir?"

• •

After securing the baggage, the man settled into the pilot's seat. He was about Ned's age. With close-cropped reddish hair and square jaw, Archangel figured him to be a former military man. The only sign of trouble was that he donned a Boston Red Sox sweatshirt. Not a good omen for a Yankee fan like himself.

Crawling into the seat next to the man, Ned extended his hand. "Phil Graham."

His new companion smiled broadly and grabbed his hand. "My name is Charlie Wainer, at your service. I am your pilot, flight attendant and mechanic."

Ned looked around the cockpit. "Is this going to get us there, Charlie?"

"Phil, you are sitting in a King Air C90B Turbo Prop. Cruising speed is two hundred eighty-three miles per hour, with a range of 1,200 miles or so. We will have to make only one stop to fill our tanks, but no one will even know. I have a secret supply in Greece that only I can find."

Charlie warmed the engines briefly and then raced down the bumpy runway. They were barely airborne when he banked sharply to the south and headed out to sea. He leveled the plane at less than a hundred feet above the surface of the water. After checking his gauges, he turned to Ned.

"We will be out of Ukrainian air space before they realize we're even here. Cross your fingers that no one else will notice us along the way. I figure it should take us about seven hours."

Ned settled back in his seat. "I thought that Marvin would meet me. No offense."

"None taken. He happens to be on the other side of the world right now, somewhere in the South Pacific. I just finished a job in Greece, so I'm your man."

"I don't know how you guys do it, flitting around the globe at will. You make it look easy."

"You don't want to know how many close calls I've had. The money is great but the risks are high. I've lost a couple of good friends in the ten years I've been doing this."

After a bit of small talk the two lapsed into silence. The vibration of the aircraft lulled Ned to sleep. He awoke only when Charlie maneuvered the plane to land at another lonely airstrip somewhere in Northern Greece, not far from the Bulgarian border. From an old rusty storage tank the pilot refilled the plane, and they were soon wending their way across the Aegean Sea.

Shortly Charlie made some adjustments to the plane's radar. He looked at Ned and remarked, "This is the trickiest part of our little adventure. We are flying between Turkey and Greece. They aren't the best of friends these days and are both a bit sensitive about their air space. I'll try to take us right down the middle.

Ned scanned the skies. "Seems like we're the only ones up here."

"Just hope it stays that way."

The weather was clear and the sea reflected a beautiful emerald tone. Occasionally they would see a fishing boat with a Greek flag waving from its stern. Ned relaxed and admired the scenic islands that passed on either side of the plane.

Just as Charlie was pointing out the isle of Santorini to their south, the aircraft suddenly shook as a military jet appeared from behind and then crossed their path. It made a quick turn, slowed its speed, and came abreast of the slower turboprop.

It was a Greek fighter. The pilot stared intently at the two of them. Charlie waved and muttered to Ned. "Wave, Phil. We're just a couple of businessmen enjoying the sights." Ned complied. The jet flew side by side with them for twenty minutes. As they entered the open Mediterranean, the pilot nodded at Charlie, tipped his wing, and disappeared.

Ned leaned back in his seat. "Can I breathe now?"

Charlie laughed. "All in a day's work, my boy. How about breaking out a couple of bottles of water and some snacks? You can be the flight attendant. Or would you rather fly the plane?"

Actually Ned could have probably handled the plane. He had flown many fixed-wing aircraft in his years with T.R.U.T.H. Today he was content just to ride.

Realizing that they were only a couple of hours from their destination, Archangel shared with Charlie the coordinates that would bring them to a spot just to the west of Alexandria, Egypt. Waiting for him there would be an Egyptian national who he himself had recruited years before to be the eyes and ears of T.R.U.T.H. in northern Egypt.

The rest of the flight was uneventful. As they neared the coast they spotted several other aircraft, some commercial and others civilian. Charlie veered slightly to the west and they strained to find their landing sight. Ned spotted an abandoned road jutting out into the desert. A lone minivan sat baking in the afternoon sun. In a whirl of sand and dust the plane came to rest about a hundred yards from the van.

Ahmed Assad had been napping. The sound of the plane's engines aroused him and he drove directly to the aircraft. Ned was already on solid ground by the time he got there. The pilot remained on board. Turning back Ned took his hand.

"Good job, Charlie. Even for a Red Sox fan."

"Red Sox? Man, I'm a Yankee fan. I won this shirt in a poker game."

So much for omens. "Your money will be in the usual place, Charlie."

"No problem, Phil. You guys always pay your bills."

Ahmed had already loaded the baggage, including the "treasure" case, into the van. On the door panels in bright lettering were the words, "Nile Tours."

Ned embraced his friend. *Isai-ak,* Ahmed?"

"I am well, thanks be to God. If you don't mind, I need to practice my English."

"Of course. How was your trip up here?"

"No problems. Once we get back on the main road there will be plenty of traffic all the way to Cairo. There are no checkpoints. They don't like to make the tourists nervous."

"Good. Let's do it!"

CHAPTER FORTY-TWO

The two men passed the time in conversation. It was the longest stretch of time that they had ever spent together. Ahmed told Ned about his wife and children, about the village where he was raised, and about his hopes for his country. Ned couldn't remember ever discussing such things with him before. Now he listened intently. It was another sign that he was changing. The ever efficient and insular Archangel was human after all. Before long he was telling Ahmed about Cheryl, and Jill, and Grace. *Gracie, hold on. I'm coming.*

It was shortly after midnight when they entered the suburbs of Cairo. Ned checked several times until the signal on the cell phone was strong enough to make a call. Then he dialed his contact for the final exchange. It appeared that he had awakened the woman who answered. She passed the phone quickly to the man whose voice Ned recognized from his previous visit.

"Who is this?" demanded the man.

"It's Philip Graham. I am here in Cairo with your merchandize."

The man's tone changed instantly. "Very good, Mr. Graham." He cleared his throat. "These are your instructions. Tomorrow at 10 am meet me at the outside café near the entrance to the Khan el-Khallili Bazaar. Do you know where that is?"

Ned was surprised. "Such a public place?"

"It is one of the busiest places in the city. No one will take notice of us."

This would not be easy. Ned tried to change the location, but his adversary was adamant. "Ten o'clock, Mr. Graham, at the café."

. . . .

It was too late to find lodging without drawing attention to himself. Ahmed suggested they park in an area near the hotels along the river, where many tour vans were left overnight. It was as good a place as any from Ned's perspective. They positioned the van so that they would be able to see any activity in the area. The young Egyptian turned the heater on high to fully warm the interior. When he finally shut the engine down, silenced enveloped them. Ned thought that this must be the quietest spot in this otherwise frenetic city.

When his friend left to find a place to relieve himself, Ned called Agent Kate Fowler, on his last cell phone. "This is it, Kate. It's time to rock 'n roll."

She sounded tired. "Ned, I have been told to give you a phone number in Cairo so that you can coordinate this with the Egyptians yourself." He jotted down the number.

"OK, do you have anything else for me?"

"The Russians have everyone in custody and are sitting on them until it's over."

"Great. And what about my ride?"

"A military jet is en-route. The Egyptians will allow it to land at Imbaba airport, a small field in the northwest part of the city. It will be waiting for you there."

"Thanks. Have the troops ready when I get home. We've got to get Grace!"

"I know Ned. By the way, your sister and brother-in-law are standing by. They trust you to do the right thing."

There was a pause. "I wish I knew for sure what that is."

• •

An Egyptian army colonel was responsible for the operation in Cairo. In Arabic he and Ned agreed upon a plan that would spread a net around the café, and at the right time would block all exits in and around the Bazaar. That arranged, there was nothing to do but wait.

Ahmed and Ned took turns napping during the night. At sun-up they found a coffee shop nearby and had some breakfast. Ned carried the heavy case with them. Ahmed had been peppering him with questions about it throughout the trip. His evasive answers did not seem to deter the curious Egyptian. Feeling he owed him some kind of explanation, Ned ordered a second cup of coffee.

"Ahmed, you are a good man and a friend. It is for that reason I can't tell you what this is about. It is better for you not to know, believe me. I can tell you that you are playing a part in making things safer for both our countries, and for the world."

His young friend grinned. Pointing at the case he said, "Can I guess?"

"No, you may not. Just help me a little while longer, and this will be all over."

With a nod he said, "As they say in your country, 'Your wish is my command.'"

CHAPTER FORTY-THREE

The Khan el-Khallili Bazaar is one of the oldest markets in the world. A mile square, it teems with merchants and tourists all day, every day. With a little bargaining "savy", one could come away with treasures of all kinds, from the typical souvenirs, to precious alabaster vases, and garments made from the finest Egyptian cotton.

Ned would have preferred a more private setting for the meeting. Despite the presence of countless police and military personnel in various forms of dress, there was still the possibility that the bad guys could find some route of escape amid the early morning crowds.

Ahmed pulled up in front of a large mosque across the street from the main market. He was to wait there for Ned to return. At just before ten Archangel waded out into traffic to meet the man whose name he still did not know. He was nowhere in sight, so Ned found a small table at the café and ordered some tea. He placed the case between his feet under the table. He felt grimy and unkempt. He needed a shave and a change of clothes. He had been wearing the same ones for a couple of days.

He glanced at his Rolex. It was now ten-fifteen. *They are being very cautious*. At ten-thirty, just as his waiter was refilling his cup, out of nowhere a man slid into the seat across from him. It was not Mr. X, but Sameer Wahed.

"So we meet again, Mr. Graham. I have come to relieve you of your burden. Just slide it over to me with your feet. Shortly I will leave and you may finish your tea."

"It's all yours," Ned replied as he pushed the heavy case under the table.

"Have you considered my proposition, Mr. Graham? We need a man of your talents, and we will pay you handsomely."

"I have your number, Sameer. Let me think about it."

"Very well then. I hope I hear from you."

Wahed rose from his chair and bodies converged on the scene from everywhere. Out of the corner of his eye Ned noticed a dozen or so persons surround a car that was idling by the curb nearby. As Wahed was being led away, a man in a sweatshirt and baseball cap introduced himself to Ned as the army colonel that he had spoken to the night before.

"Bravo. You have done your job well. May I provide you with transportation back to your hotel?"

"Thank you, but I have a ride Colonel. So I will be on my way."

Before the man could respond Ned snatched the case from the table and began walking away. The officer called after him, "I'm afraid you'll have to leave that with us."

Ned turned, stared at the man and measured his words carefully.

"Colonel, you don't need it for evidence. Your government doesn't want it in the country, and our government has the means to destroy it. You may check with your superiors but I imagine they will be very unhappy with you for delaying this arrangement."

The man's face showed confusion, and then indecision. Ned pressed the advantage.

"Was this not explained to you?"

Indecision now turned to embarrassment. It was now a matter of pride. "Of course," he muttered nervously. "But I will have to assure that it leaves with you."

Ned had to think fast. "Fine," he said. "I have hired a van to take me to Imbaba airport. I would be pleased if you would provide an escort for me there."

The Colonel seemed to regain his confidence. "I will lead the way personally."

Ned looked across the street and had a clear line of sight to Ahmed. He waved emphatically. By the time the van pulled up to the curb, the Egyptian officer had reappeared in the passenger seat of a military truck. Seated in the rear were four soldiers brandishing sub-machine guns.

"Hopping into the rear seat this time, Ned said to his friend, "Stay cool, Ahmed, and just follow that truck."

"Are we going to jail?"

"No, my friend, we are getting an official military escort to the airport.

"You still have the case…."

"You are witnessing a miracle. I am going to leave Egypt with this before they know it's gone. No one is going to get their hands on it."

CHAPTER FORTY-FOUR

You don't often hear sirens on the streets of Cairo –
many horns, but few sirens. As the mini-caravan raced
through the city, taxis, trucks and other vehicles moved aside
to create an unobstructed path. Ned smiled. It was like the
parting of the Red Sea all over again. But Moses would turn
over in his grave if he could see that it was the Egyptians
now leading the way to the Promised Land.

The airport was very tiny compared to Cairo International.
A small terminal sat at the edge of a single runway. Several
executive jets were parked off to the side. Undoubtedly this
was the place where VIP's from across the Middle East
arrived when they wanted to do business, or have a little fun,
in Cairo.

Case in hand, Ned made a personal pit stop in the terminal
as the two vehicles waited out front. Then they proceeded
directly to the end of the runway where a U.S. Navy F-18
Hornet sat poised. The Egyptian escort peeled off to the right
and positioned themselves on the edge of the runway. Ahmed
pulled right up to the plane. The pilot was standing next to
the aircraft. Above him just under the cockpit window the
name "Annie Oakley" was painted in pink.

Ned left all but the case in the van. During the trip to
the airport he went through his things and removed all of

his documents, stuffing them in his pockets. He turned to Ahmed as he reached for the door latch.

"Thank you, my brother. May God protect you….Now, get lost!"

The door was barely closed before the van turned and headed for the exit. The military truck remained in place. The pilot greeted Ned warmly. He removed his helmet and shook out a full head of silky blonde hair.

"Welcome aboard, sir. I'm Lt. Paula Buatti. I will be your tour guide for the day." She was smiling. She had seen such looks of surprise many times.

Ned recovered quickly, and shook her hand. "You're a welcome sight, Lieutenant. But you better cover that head again. We're still in Egypt, you know."

In a matter of minutes they were barreling down the runway. Ned could see that the Colonel and his men were already near the exit. They rose suddenly and he felt like he was being molded into his seat as they disappeared into the sky. When they finally leveled off, the pilot in front of him spoke into his ear piece.

"Ever ride in a Hornet before, sir?"

"Can't say that I have, Lieutenant. And please call me Ned."

"OK, sir…..Ned."

"What's the flight plan?"

"Well, sir…..er, Ned. We're flying light today. Most of our armament has been removed. We should be at top speed, about twice the speed of sound."

"How many stops?"

"This baby is a gas guzzler. We've on our way to Ramstein Air Force Base in Germany. The fly boys there will top off our tanks. Then we'll check in with my mates on the U.S.S. Nimitz out there in the Atlantic somewhere. And if all goes well you'll be having breakfast in New York at about 0900 hours."

Ned liked this woman. "I'll owe you a dinner after this, Lieutenant.

"Just doing my job, Ned. Thanks for the invite, but my fiance might get jealous."

Realizing how the young pilot had received his comment, he added, "I guess it would be hard to explain at home too."

• •

Refueling went smoothly in Ramstein. Neither of them left the aircraft. The pilot was involved the entire time communicating via her radio. Ned watched as the crew efficiently went about their work pumping hi-octane fuel into the thirsty tanks. Another airman did a visual inspection of the plane. The whole process took less than half an hour.

When they were at cruising altitude again, Paula Buatti turned her attention back to her passenger. "Whoever you are Ned, you have the whole Defense Department rooting for you. They have cleared air space for us through France and Spain so that we can make a straight shot for home."

"Be it ever so humble. Thanks, Lieutenant. You may never know what this is about, but let's just say that you're on a mission of mercy. And when it's over I would be privileged if I could really take you out to dinner with my daughter, who is not much younger than you."

"It's a date."

"And you can even bring your boyfriend."

The pilot went back to her gauges and controls and Ned's thoughts turned to his only child. Worry was a useless commodity at this point, so he tried to concentrate on what he would do when he got to New York. As long as Andropov thought the mission was unfinished he had a chance to save Gracie. If he could have willed it, the F-18 would have already gotten him there.

His ear-piece crackled and Paula's voice suddenly filled his head. "Five more minutes and we'll be on the Nimitz, Ned."

She was already positioning them for landing. As she turned he could see the speck they were aiming for in the distance. Then he lost sight of it as she lined up her approach. He felt a rapid drop and heard his companion say only, "Hold on!" before the plane touched down and was violently stopped by the arresting cables. He felt light-headed as sailors rushed the plane and opened the canopy.

Somewhat amused by the look on his face, the Lieutenant said, "Come on partner. We need a break."

CHAPTER FORTY-FIVE

Ned's progress was being relayed to Kate Fowler and the task force that had been assembled in New York. The Russian Social Club appeared normal as members moved in and out during the day. Listening devices had been lowered from an adjacent building but there was no indication yet that Grace was actually being held there. Spotters were also assigned to watch every window.

Inside the building tensions were beginning to rise. Andropov thought that he would have heard from Richard Carlson by now. His foul mood seemed to be shared by everyone else in the room. No one had slept – no one that is but Grace Dickson, who had literally prayed herself to sleep the night before. Much like her father, she viewed God as a comforting presence in her life. They would need that and more in the next few hours.

· ·

Navy showers aboard ship were supposed to be brief. Ned reasoned that he wasn't in the Navy and that he earned a good hot shower. Afterward he changed into fresh under-wear, socks, boots and a flight suit, all provided by his hosts. Some fresh fruit and a cup of coffee fortified him, and when he emerged on to the flight deck, he found "Annie Oakley" poised to take to the skies again. The Lieutenant had also showered, apparently a regulation one, because she was already in the cockpit awaiting him.

The surge that propelled them off the carrier wasn't like anything Ned had ever experienced. He couldn't decide if he was thrilled or terrified. He wasn't sure he would choose to do this again.

Both seemed to lose themselves in the gravity of the situation. The pilot's body language now suggested that she was a long distance runner straining for the finish line. Ned searched the sky and his own soul for needed courage and focus.

At twenty to nine, Eastern Time, the coastline of the U.S. suddenly appeared. Paula Buatti broke the long silence. "You awake back there?"

"I see it too, Lieutenant."

"We'll be on the ground before you know it."

She began trading responses on the radio and talked with ground control almost until the wheels screeched on the tarmac.

"Where are we?"

"At an Air National Guard base in Westhampton, Long Island, Ned. This is as far as I go." She pointed to an N.Y.P.D. helicopter sitting nearby. "I think that's your taxi over there."

Ned's body ached as he pulled his tall frame out of the aircraft. He waited for Paula to descend and then wrapped her in a big hug. She was clearly embarrassed.

"Who cares what they think," he said. "They can't begin to understand how grateful I am to you."

As Ned approached the copter, case in hand, Kate Fowler stepped out. With her was an unknown pilot and, of all people, Detective Valone, the homicide investigator who had been handling David's Hovnanian's murder.

Simultaneously, a heavily armed truck escorted by two Humvees approached them. An army officer jumped from the truck as it came to a stop.

"Sir, I am authorized to relieve you of the contents of that case."

Ned felt a sense of relief. "You're not the first one today, Major. It's all yours, but don't open it."

The exchange was made and he hopped into the copter without looking back. "I'm surprised to see you here, Detective. You haven't come to arrest me, have you?"

"Someone had to come along and protect this property of New York's Finest. It's my first helicopter ride. Actually, I have been working closely with Kate here. My bosses have allowed me to follow through with this because it will lead to our murderer."

Ned turned to Fowler. "What's the status, Kate?"

"Jill is fine. Her cabin fever has eased a bit, but that should be completely cured after a romantic dinner. The Egyptians have cracked the terrorist cell operating in Cairo. They are a little upset about your fast-talking the nuclear material out of the country. But hey, they'll get over it."

Ned was feeling impatient. "And?"

"And, as far as we can tell Andropov has no idea what has happened. We have the landlines tapped – nothing unusual there. And there has been no cellular activity in or out of there all day. I would be a little nervous if I was him. Frankly, so am I. What's the next move, Ned?"

Suddenly he felt very weary. He had been in almost constant motion for days. *You can do this, Ned Reed, A.K.A. Archangel.* He drew in a deep breath.

"OK, here we go. You may place a thousand agents around that building, but I go in alone. Understood?" The two nodded in unison. He continued. "If Gracie is there I will get her out, and then you can do your thing. If not, I will take the next step."

"What's that?" Valone asked.

Ned ignored him. He tapped the pilot on the shoulder."Go!"

CHAPTER FORTY-SIX

They landed at the municipal heliport on the East River. An F.B.I. sedan awaited them. After the three piled in, Ned instructed the driver to take them to his apartment.

"Andropov might be a little curious about my navy jump-suit," he said to his companions. "I've got to change clothes and pick up a few things."

On the way they discussed logistics. Kate had done her job well. "Ned, we have a command center set up several blocks away. When you arrive at the club we'll need a few minutes to secure the perimeter. Then it's up to you, buddy."

Archangel was totally focused now. "What can you tell me about the building?"

It was Valone's turn. "The entire ground floor is open club space. The bar is on the left when you enter. There are tables and chairs everywhere. There are a couple of couches along the back wall."

"Tell me what I don't know!"

"You have to get to the second floor. That's where you'll find Andropov, and hopefully Grace." Ned had been hoping for more information.

The car pulled up in front of his place. The others remained as he exited and bounded up the steps. It was not only a fresh change of clothes that awaited him. He knocked and stood back in full view of the peephole. A few seconds later the door flew open and Jill leaped into his arms. He carried her into the apartment, kicking the door behind him.

They embraced quietly. When they parted they burst into laughter. He looked like he had just parachuted out of an airplane. She looked like something from outer space. Dressed in one of his terry-cloth robes, her hair was in pigtails and her face was coated with some kind of green facial cream.

"I've been dreaming a lot about this moment," he said.

"You had another nightmare?"

They sat down together on the sofa. "Is it over?" she asked pleadingly.

"Almost, Jill. I'll tell you all about it soon, but right now there is one thing left to do."

Briefly he told her about Grace's captivity. He concluded by saying, "If I lose her I'm not sure I could bear it, and you wouldn't want what was left of me."

She stroked his cheek. "Go, Ned. Find her. Bring her home."

He went into the bedroom and came out a few minutes later in jeans and a sport shirt. "In his hand was the infamous little black book. "I'll be back," he said, as he grabbed a jacket from the hall closet.

"I'll be praying, Ned."

"Really?"

"Really! I have never felt this close to God in my life."

• •

The trio of Fowler, Valone and McKenna stood around Ned as they went over final details. Fifty or more law enforcement officers of various agencies stood in groups waiting for their marching orders.

All seemed to be ready. Valone turned to Ned and asked him, "Do you need a firearm?"

"No guns, no wires, no nothing. I'm going to have to talk us out of there. They are going to be looking for any reason to blow us away."

They exchanged handshakes. Ned peered at Fowler. "Tell me, one more time, what are the rules?"

"We wait until either Grace or the two of you come out the front door and then we shut the trap. If we hear nothing in thirty minutes, we send in the S.W.A.T. team."

Without replying Ned started walking away from them. It was as if his past and his future were both converging in this one moment of truth. For one last time he would be Archangel. A calm came over him and his pace quickened.

CHAPTER FORTY-SEVEN

Ned Francis Reed walked confidently through the front door of the Russian Social Club. At that time of day the only person present was the bartender who was busying himself, getting ready for the later crowd. He froze when he saw Ned, who walked briskly by him en-route to the staircase. When he glanced back, the man had the phone receiver in his hand.

They were waiting when he strode into the room. Andropov had risen from his desk. Three others had guns pointed at Ned's chest. Raising his hands, he attempted to defuse the situation.

"Relax, Sergei. It's just your messenger of good news."

One of the others moved in and patted him down. He moved away with the ledger book that Ned had put in his coat pocket. The man tossed it to Andropov. The others seemed to relax.

"Why didn't you call?" demanded the Russian.

"I only had just enough time to catch my flight. I thought I might as well surprise you."

"I don't like surprises."

"Neither do I. So where is Grace?"

He nodded to his little brother and the man opened the door behind him. Grace must have been listening, because she bolted out of the room into Ned's arms.

"Are you OK, Gracie?"

"I am now," she said.

He immediately turned to the Russian, took a piece of paper from his hip pocket and placed it on the desk. "Our business is completed, Sergei. You have your money and your precious book. This is the number of my account."

Putting his arm around Grace's waist he turned them toward the door. They took one step before Andropov stopped them. He laughed aloud. "You are going nowhere, Richard or Ned or whoever you are."

They faced him again. He was the only one holding a gun this time. Ned did not hesitate. In one motion he pushed Grace into the doorway and flipped the light switch on the wall beside them. There was an immediate explosion that lit up the room momentarily. When the light came on again, Ned was slumped against the wall bleeding heavily from his chest.

Andropov yelled at his men, "Get the girl!"

Grace was already down the stairs as the three raced one another from the room. She was half-way across the dance floor when the young bartender stepped into her path. She had the advantage of momentum and knocked him over. She pushed through the front door into the waiting arms of Kate Fowler. The four Russians also had arms waiting for them – the firearms of dozens of police officers.

Andropov heard the commotion downstairs. Ned was still conscious. "Give it up, Sergei. Half the police force is out there."

The Russian roared in anger and wildly shot off another round at Ned. This one hit his left shoulder. Before the madman could get off another shot, a burly S.W.A.T. team member appeared in the doorway and emptied a burst of automatic fire into Sergei Andropov.

• •

They would not let Gracie ride in the ambulance. The paramedics were working feverishly to keep Ned alive all the way to the hospital, which fortunately, was only minutes away.

Kate pushed the frightened girl into her car and they arrived at the Emergency entrance before the ambulance. They would find out later that the EMT's had to stop on the way to resuscitate Ned. They caught only a glimpse of him as he was wheeled through the ER directly to surgery.

They waited almost six hours. Word spread quickly about the shootout and the rescue of Grace. News trucks with giant dishes filled the parking lot across from the hospital. Jill was there in twenty minutes, and Garrett and Kara came within the hour. Some time later Anita Reed-Campbell arrived to keep the vigil for her youngest child.

The agents kept watch over them, making sure the media left them alone. Only the staff, including the hospital's chaplain, were allowed access to them. He was a mountain of a man named Roger Thaxton. His warmth and calming presence seemed to help everyone. Occasionally he would leave and return with progress reports from the OR staff. And at Jill's request, he led the group in a moving prayer as they held hands around the room.

Finally a disheveled doctor made his way into the room. Everyone held their breath. All eyes were on him.

"He's going to make it!"

Hugs and "high-fives" were exchanged before he had a chance to continue. "This is one tough man. The shoulder injury was not a big concern. The bullet went through muscle and exited the body. The other bullet just missed his heart, but severed a number of blood vessels. For a while we were putting blood into him as fast as it was escaping, but I think we have him stabilized now."

He started for the door, and then faced them again. "Is one of you Jill?"

She stood up. "That's me."

"Before we put him under he was saying your name over and over. I just thought you'd like to know."

CHAPTER FORTY-EIGHT

Archangel was dreaming...or was it a dream. He stood before the gates of heaven. John Henry Reed was there to greet him.

"Why are you here, my son?"

"To join you, father. My mission is done."

His father warmly smiled. "No, Ned, there is much more for you to do. Go back. It's not your time.....it's not your time."

The image faded, but was replaced with a succession of powerful dreams, rooted in Ned's life experiences. He dreamed in high-definition, technicolor and surround-sound. Every once in a while he would be gently interrupted by familiar voices uttering words to him or brief prayers to God.

When he finally opened his eyes he looked into the face of Jill. With great effort he spoke his first words in many days. "Will you marry me?"

• •

Jill Reed sat cross-legged in the sand under a brightly-colored umbrella. In the distance she watched her husband swimming laps in the inlet. They were on their honeymoon.

After months of painful rehab, Ned had regained his strength and muscle tone. Jill had long since buried her husband and their troubled past. Four weeks before, Roger Thaxton, the caring chaplain they had both befriended during Ned's long hospitalization, had performed two rites in the Chapel of the hospital. First there was the Christian baptism of Jill, and shortly thereafter a marriage ceremony. Witnesses to the wedding were Kate Fowler and Grace Dickson.

They had heard somewhere about this beautiful little island in the middle of nowhere. It was as if they had never been there before. Her eyes followed him as he moved up the beach toward her. He was once again deeply tanned and his hair lightened by the tropical sun. He grabbed a towel, kissed her gently and sat down beside her. They were quiet for a time. Then he nodded his head and looked at his wife.

"Let's go home, Jill. We've been here a month now. There's work to be done."

"And what might that be?"

He reached into the beach bag and pulled out a copy of the New York Times. At the bottom of the front page was a story, circled in pencil, about a woman from Kansas. She was desperately searching for her two children, who had been abducted by their father and taken out of the country.

Glancing at the headline above the article, Jill just smiled. "Oh, Oh, I'm not sure I want to know about this."

He gave her a squeeze. "Sure you do. How about we have dinner at Pablo's tonight and I'll tell you all about it?"

ACKNOWLEDGMENTS

M y thanks goes first to a loving God who has filled my life with opportunities to grow as person and to serve others on my life journey.

The editing and proofing of this book was truly a family enterprise. The heavy work was done by my English-major daughter, Julie Russell, and my Psychology-major son, Keith Nilsen. I marvel at the depth and insight of each of them. I was also helped and encouraged by my teacher-wife, Evy, and my writer-sister Valerie Mason, who shares my love of playing with words and phrases. Some of the final proofing was done by another sister, Carole Bertoldo, and my sister-in-law, Arline Brunvoll, both of whom had some useful last-minute suggestions.

Finally, my gratitude goes to the family at Xulon Press, who through all the stages of publishing, have guided this fledgling author. It has been refreshing to relate to this company whose primary focus is to nurture the awareness of God's presence in human lives.

Printed in the United States
126430LV00002B/1-123/P

9 781606 477830